DARK
SHADOWS

DARK
SHADOWS

WILLIAM BRADBURY

1603 Capitol Ave., Suite 310 Cheyenne, Wyoming USA 82001
1-888-980-6523 | admin@urlinkpublishing.com

URLink Print and Media is committed to excellence in the publishing industry.

Published in the United States of America

Library of Congress Control Number: 2024917878
ISBN 978-1-68486-884-1 (Paperback)
ISBN 978-1-68486-896-4 (Digital)

02.08.24

ABOUT THE AUTHOR

Born in January 1939 came into this world as a farm boy. Raised in southeast Kansas. He became a farm worker at the age of four. He supported himself from age sixteen on. He wanted to be a farmer, but God wanted him to be something else. He has done about every kind of work thinkable. At twenty-four he moved his family to Indiana for seven years. Michigan for twenty-five years. There he married his second wife. He became very sick and they moved to Arizona for ten years then moved back to Michigan, and Virginia for five years then back to Michigan. He has lots of short and long stories along with thirty books. Some day he will attempt to publish more of them. If they ever sell he wants the proceeds to go to help children through Missions in the U S A. He and his wife Carole the painter lives in Michigan. Grandkids are important to them. (Williamlbradbury.com)

BASIC

This is a family that is doing good until the arms of death reached into it, and takes things on a very long and hard spin for this young girl. But, in the end, she comes up with strength and happiness that she been looking for a long time. Her and her dad go through a terrible life before it ends in happiness and joy.

MEMO

This story is another dream that the writer had. Knowing it could be more than likely, and is true some place on the earth. Except this story will turn out better than if it was real life. This story will be based upon the life God had created in the beginning, and when read it may be the Grace of God helping some small girl to go forth in Gods reward system.

PREFACE

This story is about a small girl growing up with complications of her mother, and life with her dad alone. Growing into adult hood she finds a grown woman who befriends her like a mother. Her dad and her new friend's son has a lot to do in shaping her life, but they find true love and happiness ending as if the story is starting over in the end.

DEDICATED TO

All girls that God has given as gifts to their parents. That those parents will raise her in the Glory of the Lord, and teach her the foundation that God created women to do. So, she will grow up knowing the purpose God had for her when he let her be conceived in her mother's womb.

STORY PRAYER

Dear Lord, we know your will it comes from your word. and the truth of Jesus Christ your son who came to this earth as a child. We ask that you and the Holy Spirit wash the filth from girls that must go through life not knowing or living your will for themselves. A-men

SOONER OR LATER

Lula W. Koch 1892   Wilbur E. Nelson, 20th century

1. Sooner or lat-er the skies will be bright, tears will be all wiped a-way; (A-way;) Soon-er or lat-er, then com-eth the light, night will be tuned in-to day (glad day.)

2. Sooner or lat-er, our Lord knows the hour, He'll send His be-lov-ed Son; (His Son;) Sooner or later, in His might and Pow'r, Our Bat-tles all will be won. (be won.)

3. Soon-er or lat-er, yes, soon-er for some, Dark-ness will all then be past; (be past;) soon-er or lat-er our Sav-ior will come With Him will your lot be cast? (be cast?)

Chorus:

Soon-er or lat-er cares will have flown, Sun-shine and glad-ness we'll see; (we'll see;) Soon-er or lat-er God call-eth His own for-ev-er to be. (to be.)

CHAPTER 1

Down south in the small town of St. Elmo population approx. one thousand, on a very humid day in late September. Being only ten miles from the Gulf of Mexico where Tom loved to go fishing. Tom and Helen Bay were waiting for Helen's contractions to come closer together. They were expecting their first child. Tom had come home early when he got her phone call. Tom worked in Mobile and left before the traffic started to back up and now, he was waiting, if possible, for the traffic to thin out to return his trip back to the hospital. At five thirty Helen said it is time the contractions were at the time where the doctor had told her, she remembered that the first one would take longer. Tom loaded Helen into his car, and they left. The hospital should be only ten or twelve minutes from their home if all went okay.

"Tom, we have to hurry my water just broke."

"We will be there in five minutes."

Tom speed up five miles per hour.

"Tom oh! Ooh hurry up."

"There is the entrance now just hang on."

At the emergence door Tom called for a wheelchair and was waiting at the door. Helen was placed in the chair and rushed to the maternity ward and Tom went to park the car. As he entered the Hospital he asked where Helen was taken.

"Mr. Bay you have to fill out this paperwork and by then we will know which room your wife will be in."

Tom took ten minutes to prepare the papers and turned then in at the window. He was told to go to the third floor and stop at the station and they would help him to the right room. Tom arrived at the nurse station asking.

"My name is Tom Bay and I need to know where my wife is her name is Helen."

"Mr. Bay your wife is in the labor room so you can go to the waiting room area up the hallway to the right and wait someone will come for you."

"How long will it take?"

"Mr. Bay is this your first child?"

"Yes! Why do you ask."

"We can tell you only that it will take as long as it takes, but now you have to wait."

Tom went and picked a magazine to read, but he could not concentrate on anything his mind kept wondering what was taking so long. He decided that he should pray for his wife and child.

"Dear God, it is our first and we do not know just what to expect. Please help Helen to have an easy time of this birth. Help me to be patient and wait without worrying. Please let our child be safe in this process of life. Dear Jesus, help us to be good parents. A-men."

He looked at his wristwatch to find he had been setting only four minutes in the room when an older man asked him.

"Is this your, his first time?"

"Yea how about you?"

"Well, I have been here four times, and this is my fifth. I will probably be gone by the time yours arrives."

"They told me that the first one takes a long time."

"Yes, it will, my first one took five hours, and my fourth one took forty-five minutes so I will be called in about twenty minutes or less."

"Did you say five hours?"

"Yes, and sometimes it takes longer like nine or ten hours. Just set down and relax they won't let anything happen to her or the baby."

They came and told his talk partner that he now had a son and then Tom was alone again. So, he went back to trying to read to pass the time to only have his thoughts go back to why did they not come and tell him something. Then with the growl from his stomach he remembered that he had not eaten anything since noon. He walked back to the nurse station and asked.

"Do they have any place here to get something to eat, and is my wife okay it has been a long time. "

Yes, you can go back to the first floor and when you get off the elevator turn to the right and go down the hall and it is on your left. Nothing has happened with your wife the doctor is there monitoring her progress. Go and eat and take your time it will be some time, but they will call you when it is over."

Tom was hurrying down to eat not believing the nurse about the time. He was gone close to fifteen minutes when he was back asking again.

"Anything yet?"

"No Mr. Bay you need to take it easy we don't need you passing out on us, so go take a seat and try to relax. You will be notified when it is all over."

Tom set and walked and walked and he had almost watched his watch face off, and it was only eight fifteen. The door opened and a doctor walked out asking for.

"Mr. Rogers."

Tom looked around then said.

"No, I am Mr. Bay, and I am the only one here."

As he turned, he saw a man rushing down the hallway. The doctor asked him.

"Are you Mr. Rogers?"

"Yes, that is me."

"Good you now have a new baby girl congratulations."

"Thanks, boy that didn't take long when can I go see my wife and baby?"

"She will be out in about twenty minutes, and they will come for you."

Tom was asked "how long you been here?"

"Since about six o-clock."

"First time then?"

"Yes!"

"It took my wife one hour the first time, and this time she beat me. You never know when it is going to happen."

"Do you know how long the pain last?"

"Until that baby is out and breathing there is pain, but don't worry she won't remember it one hour after the time of the birth."

"Mr. Rogers, will you come with me?" said the nurse.

"Hang in there that's all you can do. You know this is a God thing he has that time all planned."

"Thanks, and congratulations on your new child."

Tom had worried himself and walked until he was bushed. Setting down and leaning back, and the next thing he knew there was a man tapping him on his shoulder asking if he was Mr. Bay.

"Yes, that is me."

"Well, it is over your wife is doing great for all the work she has went through. She is a little weak but a good night's rest, and she will be almost as good as new. Your new baby girl is one beautiful young lady, and I can tell you she is well worth the wait. You will get to see them shortly congratulations you will be proud of your wife she is a fighter."

Tom tells himself he has got to wake up so he will be presentable when he sees his new family. He is in the restroom when the nurse comes for him.

"Mr. Bay you can come with me your wife is in her room now."

"Man, this baby thing is hard on you."

"You should have been your wife if you think your part is bad."

CHAPTER 2

As the door opened Tom saw the normal hospital room there was a curtain drawn between the two beds. Half way into the room he heard his wife's voice talking to someone. The nurse stopped him and they waited then the curtain was slid back, and then he saw his wife. She looked the same except her face was puffy and a little reddish. Then he heard Helen say.

"Hi honey, come look at what we have. Isn't she beautiful?"

Tom stepped up to the side of the bed and just stood there looking at the baby that was beside his wife.

"Well you can say something sweetheart. We haven't changed much just that we are two instead of one."

"How are you? Are you okay? It took so long I was worried about you."

"I am fine I had a hard time, but I am just great now. Would you like to hold her?"

"I ah, I guess is it alright?"

"Tom, she is your daughter she will not break or fall apart."

"I believe I would love to hold her I don't want to wake her she looks like she is sleeping."

"Here hold out your arms."

Helen placed the baby into Tom's hands and watched the tears come from his eyes. For the longest time, he just stared at his baby girl not saying a word. Then he placed her back in his wife's bed and leaned over and gave Helen a big kiss saying.

"Thank you, for all the discomforting that you have been through. I want you to know just how much I appreciate your efforts, and that I love you more for doing this great thing to bring this life into the world for us to enjoy. I would like to pick you up and hold you, but I don't want to hurt you."

"That is really sweet and I love you too. Do you still want to call her Jody?"

"Yes, if it is alright with you. Jody Sue Bay I like that."

"Tom, you have to go to the station and tell them her name. Then you need to go home and get some rest we will be okay."

Tom leaned down and gave Helen a kiss and was leaving when Helen asked him.

"What about Jody doesn't she get a kiss from her daddy you know that she will remember the first kiss."

He turned and came back to the bed and bent over and kissed her on the cheek then he looked into his wife's eyes.

"Baby I am so proud of you and how you got her to be so pretty just like her mother I will never know."

"Tom, it was not me or you it was God's timing and his work through us that made her who she is."

Tom was home in fifteen minutes and knew that is was the longest ride for the distance he had traveled. He took the mail in and sorted out the junk then he went to take his bath. He was clean and all alone it was going to be a long night for him. As he lay in bed all his thoughts were towards the image of his wife and daughter. When he noticed the clock, it was three o-clock. He knew he needed his sleep he had to go to work in the morning. He tossed and turned and went to his study to read. His first thought was seeing his bible that he had not had his daily devotions. He opened it to the 127th Psalm and began to read.

"Unless the Lord builds a house, the builder's work is useless. Unless the Lord protects a city, sentries do no good. It is senseless for you to work so hard from early morning until late at night, fearing you will starve to death; for God wants his loved ones to get their proper rest. Children are a gift from God; they are his reward. Children born to a young man are like sharp arrows to defend him. Happy is the man who has his quiver full of them. That man shall have the help he needs when arguing with his enemies."

Tom looked up and thought why if I need my rest than what is keeping me awake. And why did God give me this baby girl as a reward. What have I done to deserve such a gift? Why does he want me to have many we are just now making it financially? He closed his eyes and leaned his head back. Thank you Lord for this gift I will accept it with all the love my wife and I can give to it. We will try to give back to you our reward to you for this gift by teaching her the right and Godly things she needs to know. Next Tom knew was the sun shining through the window in his eyes. He came to with a start jumping up to see that it was nine o-clock and he was late to work. If he hurried he would be two hours late so he had better call his boss and tell him he would be late.

"Hello this is Tom Bay and I am real late, and I had a bad night last night, but a good one too. We had a baby girl. I will be in, in about thirty minutes or so."

"Tom why don't you take the day off and take care of your family, and we will see you on Monday morning."

"But I need the pay."

It will be gift to you and the baby so stay and get some rest."

Helen and Jody came home Sunday afternoon and things would be different. Tom and Helen did not realize what was coming. Their sleep pattern was going to change, and they were going to get to know just how the lungs of Jody were built.

CHAPTER 3

The first week was fair and the next week was not giving any rest. Tom was worn out from not getting his sleep. Helen was irritated at Tom because she was up, and he was trying to sleep. Helen still had some difficulty moving around. Nursing the baby was not working she was not producing enough milk. That meant fixing the bottle while she nursed. She woke Tom up to fix the bottle. Tom was becoming very grouchy, and Helen was hollering at him for his help. After one week, he told Helen.

"You and the baby sleep in here and I am going to sleep in the spare bedroom. I need more sleep, or I may lose my job I cannot function like this."

Helen response was.

"Fine I don't need your help anyway I had this child, and I can take care of her by myself. You can go sleep at work if you want to and take care of yourself first."

This was there start of a family problem that neither one wanted to give into. Helen wanted pampered and Tom wanted some rest so he could support his family. After a month of fighting Helen had to give in, she knew that she would have a very hard time of doing it herself. She went to Tom late one evening and said she had decided he had been right and that she was sorry for her attitude and wanted to try and make up. After one week Tom had decided that Helen had changed. Tom's problem was he wanted to believe Helen had changed except ever now and then she got on her high horse, and it started all over again. After a while Tom became used to her actions and just let it ride until she just gave up again. It seemed that when Helen wanted sex, she was nice when it was over then she wanted all things her way. It never changed and Jody's first birthday was coming up. Helen went to the trouble of baking a cake and they made a big deal out of the occasion. Neither thinking about whither Jody would ever remember this part of her life. When the fun for them was over with Jody setting in the middle of the table with cake and frosting all over her. Tom and Helen were still laughing when Jody was tuckered out and tucked into her bed, and they were cleaning up the mess. Out of the blue Helen asked.

"Do you think it would be nice for Jody to have a little brother or sister to play with?"

"Helen as rocky as this last year has been I am not thinking about another child."

"Tom, I think we have been getting along better in the last three or four months, and I have been thinking with Jody up and walking around that if we started soon, she would be two years old by the time the next one was here."

"Her age has no design on us having another child. I would rather us begin like we were before Jody came into the picture."

"Tom, I have changed a lot you do not know what I went through with the discomforts and the pain that I had no idea what I should have been like before it happened. I want nothing more than for us to be a happy family."

"I have been praying that for some reason God could change your mood swings or help me to understand why and what I am supposed to do to accept it when it comes."

"Tom ever since Jody was born you have been in control of everything, and I just thought that you were taking advantage of me."

"Why would I take advantage of you? I know it was hard on you, but at first there was nothing I could do. You were breast-feeding Jody and that is something us men cannot do. When your milk was not enough, I fixed the bottle at night and then feed her while you went back to sleep. You could sleep anytime during the day I had to work. There was never any intention of me controlling anything. I had to work, and I could not keep up my job on three or four hours of interrupted sleep for five nights in a row. I had the lawn to mow and other things around this house and then helped you with the cooking and cleaning. I am sorry I thought for a while you thought

I was superman, or a monk all work no play no sleep. You never give me a chance until you wanted sex. Then I was a good husband but then after that short time I was back to being a no-good bum. Now you are asking me to go through that again I cannot do it. That is why I don't want another child."

"Tom what you are saying. I am sorry for that time, and I think I can change and be better the next time. I want to try, tonight, don't you?"

"Hello, did you hear anything I just said. If not, then I will tell you again next year. Maybe things will be better in my mind by then, but not before. If you still want sex, then it will be just like before with protection. I am sorry I feel this way, but you should think about what I just told you and try to understand why and how I feel this way it is not me; it is I don't want to end this marriage with another baby."

"I thought we started this so we could be a family, but it has backfired on me and you do not seem to understand or care only when you get in the sexual mood."

CHAPTER 4

The life that Tom and Helen had adjusted to was like a large roller coaster ride. Helen's mood swings did not change she was up for sex and down for most of the time. The most way was not her way, but the wants of the world were what she lived for. She had borne the pain of two miscarriages in the last eight years when the last one came she was in a place where no one could get to her, she sleeps most of the time only eating when forced to do so. Jody became her maid when not in school. Jody was angry with her mother a lot. She told her a lot of times that she was not the mother of the house. Then she paid with punishment until her dad came home. She asked her dad one day after a big fight with her mother.

"Dad why is mom the way she is all my friend's moms are not that mean and lazy?"

"Jody, I have tried to figure her out, but I come up with no good answers. I know it hurts you and I do not know what to do about it. I will have a talk with her soon."

"Dad I will be ten years old soon and I want to be a kid not a grown-up doing my mothers work while she lays in her bed. It seems the only thing she can do is work her mouth. My friends don't even want to come to my house because of my mother's attitude towards them, and me while they are here."

"Jody, I know and I have said I am sorry a lot to you. But she is your mother and I will have a talk with her. I won't say it will change things. I know part of her problem is the two miscarriages she had, but is does not take this long to grieve over the loss of a child she never saw or held in her arms. Maybe she needs some philological help, but she will not go to see anyone."

"Dad I know how she treats you and I feel like hating her, but I can't, but I don't know how you feel because of the way she treats you, and yes I know it all she tells me even about what sex is all about. I hear you both sometimes at night when I should be asleep, but I am waking up by her loud mouth."

"I am sorry I know something has to be done, but I don't want to break up this family. I still want it to work for you. As for me I am just used to it now and just push it out of my mind. I know it is hard for you, but give dad sometime to see if there is anything that can be done about your mother's condition."

"Thanks dad I love you, and all I want is some time with my friends at my house and theirs too. I can never go there because I must be here doing my work. Please before I have no friends left."

"Okay come here and give me a hug, and you go call a friend or two and I will talk to her after you are gone."

"Oh, dad you are so kind I love you, I love you, I love you, thanks."

"Don't be late so we can eat okay."

"Yes dad."

Jody leaves for her friend's house and Tom is setting thinking how to start this conversation with his wife. As he walked into her bedroom she asked.

"Now what do you want?"

"We need to talk we have a daughter who is not happy with the way things are happening in her life, and it is because of us and the way things are around here. Do you have time to discuss this?"

"I have talked with Jody now what seems to be her problem?"

"She is tired of doing all of your work while you loaf in bed. She needs time with her friends and to have them over without them thinking how bad you treat them."

"Well excuse me this happens to be our house and she has to learn how to take care of a home so she can do it someday, and her friends are a pain in the neck I told her to pick some good friends."

"Helen, I don't know what your problem is but things need to change and that seems to look in your direction. You have done nothing but complain and lay around for such a long-time Jody and

I are tired of pampering you, you need to pull your part around here and that means work. So, what is it going to be really quick?"

"It seems that you are telling me instead of asking. I don't like the way you are talking. I am your wife and you should respect and treat me better. I give you everything whenever you want it."

"That is and has not been good enough I don't enjoy you when it is only when you want me to be close to you. Once or twice a month is just not satisfactory now or in the past. I stay here so my daughter will have a home. You complain about the two children you lost. There was a reason for that I believe. The Bible says that children are a gift from God and they are his reward. I don't think that we have been or tried to do anything pleasing to God. That also includes our daughter and the way she has had to put up with your laziness."

"I don't have to lay here and take this from you. I think you are just mad because I have not given you anytime for sex. That is what, and you think about, and I don't care if I have or made love to you. How do you think I feel about you when you set out there and never come and talk to me?"

"Why don't you get your body out of this bed, and come into the house where we live you don't expect us to spend all of our time here in your bedroom watching you sleep. You are a part of this dysfunction family and we are not the ones who made it this way. Wake up before it is too late, do you hear me?"

"What you found someone else and you are now big enough to tell me about it."

"I have no one else why would I ever believe any woman who may be just like the one I already have. Our daughter is going to be ten years old next week and I want this house cleaned and available for her to have her friends over to celebrate her birthday with a party. Do I make myself clear, and there is no discussion about it, and Jody is not going to do all the prep work? If that is not good enough for you then you pack your suitcase and go to your mother's place and stay. We will and I believe I can survive without you and your complaining. What is it going to be? I will hire someone to do the work after you are gone."

"Tom I am your wife and you cannot through me out this is my home, and I am not leaving. If Jody wants a party then why didn't she come to me and say she wanted one. Besides I think you need to get some help you seem like you are mad all the time about something I never can figure out. You need to get a life and treat me like the Bible say you should. You are to love me like Jesus Christ loved the church."

"If I hadn't loved you like that you would have been gone a long time ago. Talking to you has never done any good you do not listen to anything we talk about it is all your way or no way. Jody and I don't think you are ever going to change for the better, if you don't you will be supporting yourself somewhere else."

"Tom please do not talk like that I love you and I want to do right. I have these thoughts that keep me depressed most of the time, and I really want to do different but I don't seem to get passed or better with just myself."

"Do you want a shrink to talk to?"

"No I am not crazy it is just I wanted more children and I have not been able to carry them. I will get over it."

"It has been over one year since the last time and that is more than enough time for most people. What is it going to be you or I hire someone and Jody is not going to do the work while, you, boss her around. I need an answer now?"

"Tom I will do it and I want you now can you come over here?"

"No I have work to do in the yard and Jody is gone to her friends."

"But I want you now?"

"Not going to work this time you are going to start doing instead of getting your way."

"Tom if I need you tonight will you come to me?"

"No I want a wife and a family not a sex goddess who cares only about herself and her feelings."

Jody got her tenth birthday party. Her mother did as she was told. She cleaned the house, and baked the cake even brought Jody a gift. The party was good it helped change the minds about her mother the old grouch. Helen was the life of the party. When the girls all had left, Helen went to Jody and told her.

"Now you have had your fun and it is your mess and you will clean it up."

"Why are you this way? You could be a fun mother, but you are a fake this is your house you want it cleaned up now you clean it up. If you want my help you ask for it."

Without thinking Helen hit Jody with a backhand across the mouth cutting her lip and the blood started running. Tom walked in to see Jody crying to ask.

"What is wrong?"

Then he saw the blood. He bent down to see and Jody told him.

"Mom hit me."

"She had it coming she has got to quit sassing me I asked her to help clean up this mess and she told me if I wanted it cleaned up I could do it myself. She is not going to get away with sassing me like that."

"Dad she told me it was my fun mess and I was going to clean it up it was her house."

"Helen, we just talked about this a little while ago like last week. Do you think we are going to buy this with you taking your hate out on me and your daughter?"

"She needs to show a little respect I am her mother and she will do as I say or she will get punished. I will no longer tolerate her attitude towards me like she has been showing. I am going to my room she can clean up this mess all by herself now."

Helen stomped off to her room.

"Jody come let's clean up your mouth and see just how bad it is."

"Dad I can take care of it I don't think it is really bad it will just be sore for a while."

"Okay I will help you with the clean-up and then we need to talk."

"Okay dad thanks I love you."

"I know and I am still sorry about your mother we will discuss when we are through."

Jody went to clean up the blood and cry because she had hoped the last week was something that could be a new life with her mother and dad and that would make her life much easier.

"Dad see." As she pulled her lower lip down. "It is just a small cut."

"I see I just wanted to know if it needed some doctoring, but I think it will take care of its self. You look like you were crying did it hurt that much?"

"No, it was because of the way mom acted I just do not understand. Maybe she needs Jesus in her life."

"Maybe she needs to go back and get Jesus in her life where she left him a long time ago. Maybe that is part of her problem, but she will say that is not true we have talked about it, but she does not want to listen. Jody come let's go to my study and talk about the rest of our life."

Jody set on the couch beside her dad, and he put his arm around her.

"Okay dad, tell me what is going to change for us?"

"Jody, would you be upset if your mother did not live here for a while."

"What do you mean not live here?"

"I am going tonight and ask her to leave and go spend some time with her parents up north. I need to get some happiness in your life and mine. I want us to have something besides havoc we need to come home to a happy house so we can be happy in our hearts. Jesus does not want to live in an unhappy home, and I know now it is up to me as the head of this house to make this home a happy place not only for us, but for Jesus to live in. I have given up trying to make your mother happy. I don't know what to do anymore. I have prayed for this for so long and nothing has changed. I now think Jesus wants me to step up and be counted for what the Bible tells me to do. I think that the Devil is here and I need to remove his source for staying. If your mother ever changes her mind and wants to come back a changed person then we will take her back, but only if she wants to be happy with us. If not then we will make it on our own. Does that make you afraid if so I need your input it is for you I will do this not for me."

There was a long silence before Jody spoke.

"Dad I don't want her to leave but I also don't want her to stay like she is. I don't want to be talked about like the kids who live in homes with no mom or dad. I know you are unhappy and so am I, and if this is the only way then I will agree with you, and except what becomes from your decision."

"Thank you for your honesty and it will take some doing but if I have a hire someone to come occasionally to help then I will do that I want you to be a happy child and live in a happy home as best I can make it. I want you to be a child for as long as you need to be one, I know this is going to be hard for you, but it will be hard for me to live without a woman in my life also, but I believe we are both strong enough to make it. Do you, are you sure you want to try with me?"

Again, Jody was thinking for a long time then looking at her dad and putting her arm around his neck said in his ear.

"I can try."

"That is good enough for me."

"Good then I am going to talk to your mother, and help her on her way. Tomorrow is Saturday and she will be put on the bus and we will say goodbye. Go and try to get some sleep, and always remember I am doing this because I think we need it. I hope that God will understand why this is happening."

CHAPTER 5

Tom went to Helen's bedroom and closed the door. "What do you want I didn't ask you to come to me?"

"We talked about this over a week ago and I thought it may have soaked into your head what was expected of you, but I see it was just a delusion to us. Now you have only one choice and we are making it for you. Tomorrow you are getting on a bus and going to your mother's house for a while or a long time. Jody and I have decided we want somewhat of a happy home and we do not get it with you here. There is going to be no arguing or back talking. I am sorry you can't seem to get it or don't care one way or the other, but we are feed up with your actions."

"Tom, you can't just kick."

"I said end of story we have tried for so long at it and it is not working. It does not register with your brain tomorrow is it pack your clothes you will need and I will take you to the bus station. Good night. We might regret this but right now we want out of this trap we have been in for so long."

"Tom!"

Is all Helen got out of her mouth before the door slammed closed? She decided that she was not going alone she would take her daughter with her. She would pack her things and then go talk to Jody about going with her. When she was through packing, she went down stairs to find there was nobody home. They must have gone to eat somewhere. Helen decided tomorrow morning would be soon enough and went back to her room. Helen heard them come in and talk for a while then they went to each other's rooms. She waited for one hour then got up and went to Tom's room touching him on his shoulder to wake him.

"Tom this is Helen I need to talk to you will you listen?"

"The answer is no I am tired of this game you play, and we do not know the rules. Go back to your room and leave me alone."

"I come in here to see if I could make love to you don't you want too?"

"Go away now and leave me alone."

Helen said some bad words and left she went to Jody's room to find the door locked. The next morning at seven o-clock she was awaken and told she had one hour to get ready so he could take her to the bus station. Helen got dressed and then went and tapped on Jody's door waking her up and telling her to get dressed she only had one hour before they had to leave. I will help you pack if you want me too."

"I am not going anywhere and if you don't get out, I am going to call dad in here."

"Jody why are you so mad at me you act like you hate your mother?"

"I am not mad, and I don't hate you I just do not understand why you have to be the way you are. None of my friend's mom's treats then the way you treat me. I can tell you I love you, but I do not feel it now. Now goodbye and tell grandma and grandpa I said hello and I love them."

Jody turned over and pulled the covers over her head. Helen left the room knowing she had lost her daughter and her husband, but she was not through yet. Tom took her bags to the car telling her.

"It is time to go get in the car we are not going to be late you will be on the bus some way or the other."

Helen walked through the house as if she really missed the place and went to the car. Tom started up and drove off to the bus station saying nothing all the way. After arriving at the station and before Helen opened her door she asked Tom.

"Tom is this goodbye forever, and why don't you love me anymore?"

"I am sorry I am going to tell you the last time I love the woman I married so long ago and you are not that woman anymore and have not been for a long, long time, now out of the car I have your tickets."

"When can I come back?"

"From what I just told you, you figure it out, and until you do, do not call us we will not talk to you, why because it has not done any good and it is up to you to prove you want it bad enough, or not at all."

"Well, you can leave now so I won't hurt you anymore."

"I will leave when you get on that bus and it is on the road."

"Can I give you a hug and kiss goodbye?"

"No go get on the bus."

Tom waited for the bus to leave and as it pulled out into traffic, he has this very deep sickening feeling in his gut, but he would get better he had Jody to take care of and try to figure out just how he was going work it out. Nothing would probably change he had done the shopping and most of the cooking and a lot of the laundry for years. As he drove out into the traffic he told himself.

"What are you so sad about life could be better or worse it would be up to him to make it."

Tom and Jody went on with their lives and Helen never called. Jody was so much a different child she was happy, and her friends were over a lot especially on weekends. Tom was happy he didn't have to work all day and come home to the many different moods swings that his wife had put on him. He missed the sexual part of life, but it wasn't that good or frequent when Helen was here and decided she wanted it. He could live without it all he wanted was his daughter to have a happy life. Helen had been gone a long-time Jody would start high school in the fall. She had blossomed into a very beautiful girl. Her and her dad had talked about all the things about life even the birds and the bees. Jody loved her dad, and they spent time doing things together. They enjoyed there one night out to eat and a movie. They went to the mall one night each week and to church every Sunday. They cleaned the house together, cooked and done the dishes together. Three Fridays a month Jody had one of her friends over. They enjoyed playing games after dinner and got to stay up until midnight never having to be told lights out. Jody started playing basketball and volleyball. She became good enough to be one of the starting team players. During her sophomore year, some of her friends started dating and her Friday nights became far and in between. Tom asked her one Friday night.

"What happened to all your friends are they too busy to be friends anymore?"

"No dad they are all dating on Friday night."

"Do you think you should be dating also?"

"No, I don't want no boys hanging all over me like they do my friends. I have other things I would rather be doing, but I miss the fun we used to have on Friday nights, don't you?"

"Well can we do something about it, what would you like to do?"

"I don't know, now, I just miss the time with the girls when we use to study and play together, but mostly the talking."

"Well, if you come up with something you let me know I am very flexible and your happiness is all that matters."

Tom went to all of Jody's games in town or out of town. He was very proud of what his daughter could do on the court she was just good. He was waiting for her to come from the showers so they could go home. When she came out his eyes went to her, she was just a beautiful girl that was going to be sixteen years old soon. When she came up to him, she said.

"Dad, I want you to meet a new student this year is that okay?"

"Sure, where is she?"

"She is a he and he is right over there."

She was waving for Bill to come over to them. When he arrived, he stood taller than Tom by about three inches.

"Dad this is Bill Day he is one of the basketball players on the boys' team. Bill this is my dad, Tom."

"Pleased to meet you, Bill."

"Same here do you come to all of Jody's games?"

"I wouldn't miss one for nothing."

"Dad we can come and watch the boys play for our Friday night thing if it is okay with you."

"Well, I don't see anything wrong with that it would help boost the school for us to be here I think that is a great idea."

"Bill, see you tomorrow have to go and get my beauty sleep."

"Jody, you have had plenty of that already." Tom said "A-men to that."

On the way home Tom never mentioned Bill and Jody didn't either. They just talked about her game, and Tom brought up that in two weeks she was going to have a very special birthday.

"What would you like to do sixteen is the first milestone that we have in life so I want to make it very special for you, you think about it and let me know."

"Okay dad, give me a couple of days and I will tell you what would make it special for me."

Jody never said anything about it until after the Friday night game that they went to see the boys play.

"Dad I well I, let's talk about it tomorrow after breakfast."

"Okay with me you lovely thing. I want you to know that God must of thought I was something great to give me such a smart lovely and beautiful daughter as a reward for living. I cannot thank him enough for you. You make me very proud just too be around you and what you have made of yourself. I love you Jody and some day you will be gone to college or even married to some good-looking guy, and I will be alone that is the day that will make me sad yet so full of joy for you."

"Goodnight dad I love you more than any other person or thing that God has put into my life."

"Thank you, dear child good night."

Saturday morning Jody cleaned up the table and set back down.

"Dad ah, I would like to have a party and invite my girlfriends and their boyfriends over for just some cake and ice cream and fun. I want to do this so you can see just how they have changed in the last year since you have seen them."

"I think I and you would like that very much. You pick the day and tell me how many so I can get a cake large enough. I will need probably a week for the cake Okay."

"I will let you know by Wednesday next week and then, and then we can have it in two weeks from today in the afternoon unless you have something going on that day. Well, it is your day so I will save that day the same as the day you were born. Just give me the count as soon as you can."

"Thanks dad, now we need to start the cleaning process it should not take long. In two days, the house was clean and it looked great. The cake is ordered and the ice cream is in the freezer. The next Tuesday Jody tells her dad.

"I have asked six of my girlfriends and they are bringing their boyfriends so I think there will be with us fourteen or maybe fifteen people. Who may show up or not show up. I want to ask you if I can ask Bill to come if he can I have not asked him yet."

"Jody, you tell him that he will never be invited to a more beautiful sixteen-year-old girl in his lifetime."

"Dad, I cannot tell him that he is just new and I want him to get to know some of the other kids in school."

"I was just kidding I would not say anything one way or the other about him showing up at my daughter's birthday party he would be just a friend of yours to me as long as he keeps his hands in his pockets."

"Dad!"

"Okay I am just making fun."

Everything is settled everything is in place and the party is just one hour away from starting soon the kids will be showing up.

"Dad before anyone comes, I really want to thank you and appreciate what you do for me. I want to thank you and God for letting you be my dad. Nobody could have a better dad then I have."

Thank you, my dear, having someone like you makes it easy to be a dad."

The doorbell is ringing, and Jody says,

"I will get it."

As Jody opens the door there is a strange woman standing there.

"Well, are you going to ask me if I came for your birthday, and I have something very special for you."

"Dad someone here for you I think."

"Jody this is your mother can I come in?"

"Helen what are you doing here you were told to stay away. Now you show up to spoil Jody's birthday party you are not welcome in this house. You have had no connection with her for over six years. Now you show up to what spoil her very special day. I am asking you to leave now or I will have you removed before her friends show up."

"Jody, don't you want my present I brought it special, and your grandma helped me?"

"I don't know you; you do not remind me of my mother, and like my dad said I don't want nothing from you on this day."

"But I am your mother and I care about you still; mothers cannot forget about their daughters."

"I don't have a mother that I can relate to so you can now leave my friends will be here in ten minutes or less. Dad make her go away."

"You heard my daughters wish, now will you leave and don't come back until you have full filled what we talked about when you had to leave."

With that Tom closed the door.

"Dad, she has more nerve than a cornered skunk what made her think she could just show up without being invited."

"Jody, she is gone I want you to go and freshen up and get back to your lovely self. Please do not even think about her and what she just did I want you to enjoy yourself with the people you care about the most this is your special day and I demand that you enjoy it to the fullest you can. Now hurry I hear voices I will get the door until you get back hurry! Hurry!"

Jody's sixteenth birthday was a rewarding success Jody spent a lot of time with her friends and Bill talked a lot about his life to Tom. When they had gone, Bill was the last to leave.

"Tom, I want to thank you for your time and hospitality."

Then he turned and just said.

"Thanks Jody, I did enjoy myself. Again, thanks for asking me today."

CHAPTER 6

Tom and Jody were just about through with the clean up after the party when the doorbell rang. Tom being closest he opened the door.

"Hello Tom, I have come back after they all left, and I want to talk to you and Jody."

"Like I said do not ruin this special day for Jody."

"I want to talk to you about what you told me I had to prove before I could come back, and that is why I am here besides to give this gift to my daughter. May I come in and explain?"

"It is four o-clock, and we must be somewhere at six o-clock. You can have one hour and if Jody wants that gift, then it will be up to her, and if not then you can take it back."

"To start with I want to tell both of you that until I arrived at my mother's house, and she said one month then you can get your own place. Did I realize just what I had lost? I needed someone to feel for me, but there was no one around after one month without work and having to move out I found a woman at one of the bars that said she would help me. I became a prostitute for one whole year always looking and asking for help from some man I had to be with. One year later one man was kind enough to give me a job. I started cleaning restrooms at the factory he worked at. I found myself in the sewer and then cleaning the sewer and knew I could go no lower in life. I felt obligated to that man, but after one year I found other work, I did not have to clean the sewer of life, but I was still in the sewer because I needed the money to live. Two years later a man asked me to move into his house. I knew that was a way to also move out of the sewer to something closer to what I had lost. After one year, he asked me why I did not divorce you and marry him. I told him to give me time. He waited six more months and asked me again. This is what I told him. I ruined my marriage my husband Tom and I could not divorce him until I proved that I was one that was wrong, and that over time I could show him that I was now changed. I asked him to wait until I could face you and tell you this. He agreed and paid my way here so I can come clean and tell you I have chosen a new and better life. Not to hurt you or make you feel bad I am still your wife and it is my responsibility to do as you asked six years ago. To you Jody I am truly sorry that I did not know how I could have inflicted so much pain on you and that my actions would send so many deranged thoughts in your mind. I only ask that you could forgive me for all that I at the time either did not realize or did not care because of the disrupted mind that I had. You Tom if you can forgive me I will except it if you still want me then it would take time and break the man that has stood by me for all this time. If you want a divorce, I will not contest it. I know all that has happened in my life for the last fifteen years is no one's fault but my own. This I will have to learn to live with somehow."

"You say you are my mom, and can I forgive you for what you did to me. I can because Jesus tells me to do so. You are forgiven. If you want me to accept your gift, I will do that, but I will not open it in front of you. Will I accept you as my mother I have no choice. Do I want you in my life now the answer is no. If you want to be my mother, then you will have to prove to me that you are good enough to be my mother. What you and dad does have nothing to do with you being my mother now. Thank you for the gift but now I must go and make myself presentable for this evening."

Jody got up and left the room leaving the gift setting on the table where it was placed when Helen came into the house.

"Tom, will you give me your answer I know you have to leave before long."

"I don't believe I can ever ask you to come back. You have a new life, so I believe that is where God wants you. If you want a divorce so you can marry this man, then go and get it I will not contest it and I will not be there when it happens. You will get nothing from this house or from me, nor your daughter. If that is clear, then you may leave.

"Tom, I know I hurt you and Jody very much and I can only say that I am sorry."

"Sorry is a game that kids play I do not believe you anymore when you say it."

Helen got up and left the house without another word. Tom and Jody finished up the day at the most prestigious restaurant in Mobile. They returned home at midnight to end her sixteenth birthday with a day she would remember forever. As they entered the house Jody walked past the table where the gift set that her mom had brought her. She decided it was time to see what she had received. All the time while she was unwrapping the gift she kept thinking if it was something just to upset her. After she had the wrappings off she noticed only picture frames so it looked. When she turned the first one over there was a note saying these pictures of me one for each year I have been gone so as for you to remember what I had changed into over the years I have been away. I am sorry for this time in our lives that you needed a mother more than any other time and I was not there for you. I would like to have seen you your face when you looked upon these pictures, and by now I already have, or I will never see. Again, I am sorry for this time in our lives I know it was all my entire fault, and I have no other one to blame but me. I know your dad tried and even though I knew I loved him more than anything on this earth. I can only look at myself for the remorse and stupidity I put you both through. I know that you are one beautiful girl from the pictures you sent grandma and I know that I may never see you again in this life here on earth. I will pray for you always. I hope you had a very happy sixteenth birthday. And may you have one just like it each day of the rest of your life.

CHAPTER 7

"Dad why would she do this, just to make me feel bad or does she think I have really missed her."

"Sweetheart you are halfway through your teen years you have come a long way, but you have a long way to go. Do not let things like this upset you. You have choices to make you will feel better if you pray about this and then do as you think is right. I cannot make this judgment for you. If you let God perform in your heart before you decide you will always feel better later. Let Jesus take the burden from your heart, and he will carry it to where it needs to be, and you will feel blessed for letting him carry it for you. I will say nothing if you want to keep these pictures it is your decision. She is no longer a part of my life, but she will always be a part of your life. Someday you and your mother just may re-counsel back to meaning something to each other and make a mend to live with something or some feelings towards each other. I will never be able to make you feel how sorry that you of all people had to go through what you did when you were so young. After ten years of great heart aches and great pain I had to decide that not only hurt me, but also hurt you for more years than I would ever be able to live. That may have been selfish on my part, but I needed to change, and it was breaking my heart to see you treated so, and for being a young child expecting to be all grown up by your mother. That is pain I will live with all my life even if I decide to look for another woman to spend my last years with after you have left the nest so to speak. I know I will lose you some day, and it will all happen on just that one-day. I know that I will always have your love and concerns for me, but you cannot stop your life just because of me."

"Dad, I don't think I will ever leave you, but I know someday I will have to. I know I will never find a man who cares or loves me the way my dad does. I will not be looking for him anytime soon either."

"Sweetheart I want to tell you something. Dads hold our hands for a little while and holds our hearts forever. Now what about this new boy, Bill is it, he seems such a nice boy and having to leave all his friends so far away and just start over. I want to tell you how nice you have been to him as a friend to help him get adjusted to his new life. What I am saying someday one just like him will come and run into you, and in a short instance, and the blinking of your eyes he will be there because God has placed him there. At that time, all your love and thoughts about your old dad will change before your eyes. I know that sounds strange to you, but you cannot stop or change the plans of God. He put that into this lovely body and mind of your way before you were born. You will forget and take the path he had planned for your way before we knew you were coming. This is not to scare you, but it will happen before you can change it, it will be the same as when you accepted Jesus into your heart as your savior. I pray that God has the right time and place for this to happen for you as we say in human terms."

"Dad, I will never leave you alone."

"I know but you need to get on your knees and then get to bed you know it is one o-clock in the morning."

"It is okay I could talk with you forever you are so wise beyond any of my thinking. I love you and I love God for giving me to only you, and just maybe someday I will realize that I do have a mother. Good night dad."

Jody took the pictures to her room and stored them under her bed. Now, they were just dust collectors. She lay in bed for a long time thinking why this had happened. For what purpose did this happen what could she become because of it. This was all a very dark mystery to her. Her biggest thoughts were would it affect her later if she even got married being scared, she would be like her mother. Yet she had been thinking a lot about her new friend Bill Day. She wondered what kind of life he had grown up in. Did she dare to ask him just being a new friend of three months. What would he think would he believe she was leading him into something or just keep away thinking she was to nosy, or just like all the other girls. She would talk it over with her dad first to get his perspective on such a subject she didn't want to hurt or be hurt over something of little values for her age. Even though she was noticing other girls looking and talking about Bill. Maybe she would ask around to see what their intentions were before she fronted Bill about what he was thinking or if he was even thinking at all. Then she came to thinking I need my sleep more than worrying about what others thought about a certain boy that was already her friend.

CHAPTER 8

It was Saturday morning the sun was up and shinning. The birds were singing, and Tom had an idea. He was going fishing. But he didn't want to go alone. He was setting at the table finishing his coffee. Jody came through the door rubbing the sleep from her eyes.

"Daddy you are up early today, aren't you?"

"Yea a little, but I wake up with great ideas, then decided I didn't want to do it alone."

"What great idea did you have so early in the morning?"

"I would like to go to the gulf and go fishing, but I have decided not to go because I would be all alone, and it would be to be boring."

"Would you like me to go with you?"

"I was thinking maybe you could ask Bill your friend if he would like to go with me."

"If you want, I will call him and ask if he would, but I don't know if he likes fishing or not."

"I would like it if you would do that and if you know where he lives, I could pick him up."

Jody goes to the phone and calls Bill.

"Hello Bill."

"Just a minute."

"Hi this is Bill."

"This is Jody and my dad asked me to call you and see if you would like to go fishing down in the gulf."

"Oh, wow I would love to go with your dad are you going too? Hey mom can I get off to go fishing with Jody's dad down at the gulf. Jody, are you going with him?"

"I don't know he did not ask me to go he wanted to take you fishing."

"When or what time does he want to go?"

"He said he would pick you up so knowing him it will be within the half hour. Will that be okay with you?"

"I will be waiting for him."

"Dad Bill said he would be glad to go with you. He seemed excited."

"Then I will get things loaded while you get ready."

"I ah you want me to go too?"

"Unless you would rather not then you can tell me just where Bill lives and stay home."

"I forgot to ask where he lives, I will call him back."

As Jody waits for Bill to come on the line, she gets a big smile on her face. Thinking why my dad would want to take this strange boy fishing.

"Hello this is Bill what can I do for you?"

"Bill, Jody again I forgot to ask where you live so dad can pick you up."

Bill gives her his address and she hangs up.

"Dad, I think I would like to get out so if you want, I will go with you I can set and read it will be better than hanging out here all alone."

"Did you get his address?"

"Yes, I can show you how to get there I will be ready in a jiffy."

"You do not need to get all prettied up just come in your natural state we are just going fishing."

"Okay dad I will look, I will look like I just got up."

"I mean wear some jeans and tennis shoes not a pretty dress."

"I love you dad."

As they drove towards Bill's home Tom asked.

"Does Bill have a dad if so, maybe he would like to go with us?"

"I don't know we have never talked about it, and I have never met his parents. That would be nice if he could go. It would give you old men something to talk about."

"Why young lady what do you mean old men."

"Dad, we missed our turn that was their street."

"Well, there is no traffic so we will just back up and turn. Us old men don't read street signs like young girls do. Especially when we don't have the directions and are depending on you to read them for us."

"I am sorry dad I was talking instead of paying attention. There it is the one with the black trim on the right."

Bill is waiting on the porch and gets up and picks up his tackle and rod. As he turns and waves to his mother before he enters the car.

"Hi Jody and Mr. Bay, it is great that you asked me to go fishing with you."

"Young man is your dad home, and would he like to go with us he is welcome and we can wait."

"I have no dad me and my mom live with no one else."

"Sorry to hear that."

"That is just the way it is."

"Was that your sister at the door?"

"No that is my mother I have no other siblings."

"Well, she is one pretty mother and looks so young."

"Yea my mom is thirty-eight going on eighteen."

"Before we go dad, can we meet her Bill?"

"Sure, I will go get her she is just a country girl living in town."

"Mom this is Jody the one I told you about that has become a good friend and showing me around school and this is her Dad Mr. Bay. My mom Alice Day. Please to meet you Mrs. Day we will take good care of this lad we will be back around four thirty or five hopefully with some fish to eat."

"Nice to meet you Mrs. Day." said Jody as they returned to the car.

"Well relax kids we have about twenty minutes to get to a good fishing place. Bill where does your mother work?"

"She does hospital billing records out of our house. So, she works at home."

"Well, that is neat something new I have never heard of that before."

"She worked at the hospital where we used to live up north until Dad just disappeared and she had such a hard time of it they told her to move down here, and she could do her job from home. She does it all on a computer and fax line."

"Well, I need a job like that."

"It has been hard for us we left all of our friends, and they don't know where we live so I was happy your daughter befriended me at school. It is kind of hard for me to meet and make friends. I hope our past will stay behind us my mom never goes any place just stays in the house even I go to the store for her."

"That's too bad she seems such a nice person."

"Yes, but very hurt now."

"Well let's catch a big fish and see if that will cheer her up some."

They spent five hours fishing and playing in the sand. They had fun Jody was talking and fishing with Bill they were carrying on like brother and sister while dad was catching all the fish.

"Hey, you two if you paid more attention to them fishing poles you could catch more fish."

"Dad we can have fun and fish at the same time."

"Yea if you don't catch any fish, I get to eat mine all by myself."

Bill thought Tom was serious, so he told Jody.

"You finish the sandcastle, and I will catch some fish so we can eat some too."

"Okay big brother go and do what daddy says and I will play in the sand."

"Ha! Ha! What is this big brother stuff."

After Bill had caught two fish Tom told them they could go now that they had their limit even though I did most of the catching lets load up for home. We are going to have Bill back later then what we told his mother."

At Bills house his mom said.

"Come on in I have fixed dinner for all of you."

"Why that is just okay, but we have got to get home and clean these fish."

"Come and eat Bill is good at cleaning fish he can help."

Tom and Jody agreed so they washed up and set down to eat.

"Bill, would you pray for this time together and this meal for us."

"Sure! Dear Heavenly Father I want to thank you for looking over my mom and I all this time. And for the good friends, that you have brought my way. Thank you for Jody and her father for asking me to go fishing with them and the great time we had. Thank you for the fish that Mr. Bay caught. Thank you for this food you have provided for us and for the work that my mother did for us to eat and nourish our bodies. Thank you for your son that you gave to us. We love you Jesus and in your special name we thank you and praise you A-men."

They had a great time during dinner. After wards Tom and Bill went out back to clean the fish. The big ones they flayed and the small one they left whole without the heads. Tom gave Bill and his mom one half of the fish, and they were on their way home.

"Dad, Bill's mom seemed like she was a little afraid of something she did not talk very much."

"Why do you think that I heard her say quite a lot and we forgot to thank her for our dinner. When we get home, we must call and take care of that she may think we were very rude since we did not know them very well."

"Hi, Mrs. Day, this is Jody and I called to thank you for dinner we forgot to do that, and dad felt bad, so I am calling to thank you and Bill for your hospitality."

"Well thank you Jody maybe we can do it again some time and eat the fish you left us. I liked your dad he seemed right at home; I mean he didn't seem very nervous about being here."

"Believe me he was nervous, but he has a way of keeping it inside."

"You have a caring handsome father."

"Thank you Mrs. Day I can tell you; you are very nice and really a beautiful person for your age, and to let you know my dad said so a lot of times today."

"Well, you tell him thanks for the nice compliment. And for taking Bill fishing he has missed that since his dad left."

CHAPTER 9

Jody had finished her sophomore year and she and Bill had both done well in their sports. They had never dated unless you would call studying together such. Bill had gotten closer to some of the boys on the team he played on. He was a shy boy not wanting to get involved with any one so no one could get close to him except his mom. Jody thought he had a mystery about him but would not ask because it may break up their friendship. During the summer, they did not see each other. Jody was just staying home and her and her dad did something as whatever. Bill had a summer job that kept him busy. The summer days most of the time was just too hot and humid for just having fun. When school started Bill had football and he was going to be the starting quarterback. The last year he only played in three games for a short time each. Now it would be up to him to help his team win. Jody was asked to be a cheerleader so she went for it they would be at the game anyway. It had become one of the things that Tom and Jody did all school year. Now that Bill was the starting quarterback, he soon got his mom to come watch. When Jody saw her at the first game, she went to say hi telling her.

"My dad is setting over there why don't you go set by him he would like that."

She told Jody that she didn't want to be noticed. So, Jody left it at that for the first game then she told her dad.

"Why not go set by Alice she was all alone and needed some company."

"I will go say hi and see if it would be alright with her maybe she needs company and maybe she does not want any."

Tom went around the bleachers and climbed up to where Alice was setting.

"Well, hello it has been a long time since I have seen you, how have you been?"

"So, So, I guess just working all the time. You seem happy and about the same."

"Yea what you see is me. Is or are you setting with someone?"

"Oh, no I just came to see Bill play he has been after me for all last year so I told him I would come and watch his home games this year. I have so much to do on the last day of the week it is hard for me to just get up and leave. I don't know anything about this sport, but I know he tries to do his best."

"Bill is as good as anyone I have seen since Jody, and I have been coming to watch. That has been our thing since she started high school. This year I must set alone since she started cheer leading."

"So, we are both alone maybe we could set together. I am kind of a loner now. My interest is to see Bill get through school and make enough to send him to college."

"You sound like Jody and I that is our goal. Now that she does not set with me, I get kind of lonely. I stay away from the rowdy kind that is why I set by myself."

They watched the game without much talking until half time when Tom excused himself to go get a drink asking if Alice wanted a soda or some water.

"No, I did not bring my purse so I don't have any money with me."

"How about I repay you for the dinner you fixed us."

"Okay I like sprite if you insist."

"Anything to eat like a hotdog or popcorn?"

"Oh, no I never snack just eat at mealtimes."

"I can tell by the shape you are in; I will be right back."

Tom was gone and while waiting in line he could not forget the smell of her perfume and wanted to kick himself for what he had said about her figure. He needed to apologize to Alice for his remark.

"I am back and here is your soda. Alice I am sorry for what I said about your shape, but to a man you are in great shape. I just want to tell you that maybe to beef up your morel about being out in public."

"Thanks Tom, but I keep my guard up to shield myself from being hurt."

"Believe me I would never hurt you in any way. I would or I have needed a friend and I see the way Bill and Jody are, and I miss having someone just to talk to, occasionally. How about you?"

"Yes, but I have to be careful about being seen in public."

"Would I be out of line if I asked why. You seem to me to be a very nice, beautiful and lovely woman and you have a son that has had some good upbringing, and if you don't want to tell me I well understand. The reason I am asking is that you said you only would come to Bill's home games. I was going to ask you if you wanted to go with me to his out-of-town games I would be glad to take you to see them."

"Why would you want to do that?"

"Just to have a friend is my only position. I want you to know that only God will show me the next woman that he wants me to be interested in or involved with in any capacity other than a friend."

"Okay for one time I will by it. But please do not ask about my staying at home life I have a very good reason for doing it."

"Okay you go with me to the ball games, and I won't ask you about your home life."

Tom and Alice went to all the football games even Bill and Jody did not know they were going together to the games. After the last game of the season Tom asked Alice if she would like to come to Jody's seventeenth birthday party, I think she asked Bill to come, and you could come with him. You do not have to bring anything but yourself and we do this in a dress down mode only."

"I will see if I can get my work done on time and I will let you know. I will probably have Bill tell Jody at school."

"That will be okay it is hard for an old man to be the only adult at a young kid's birthday party. We do not talk the same language."

"All I can say is I will try, and I will let you know. Thanks for thinking of me anyway."

One week passed and no answer from Alice. That evening he talked to Jody about having a party for her on her seventeenth birthday.

"Dad I am not a kid any more you don't need to have a party for me."

"I know that, but you will always be my little girl so let me do it because I want too."

"Bill told me today that his mom could come to your party if she knew the day and time. When did you ask her? Are you interested in Bill's mom?"

"Only as a friend nothing else."

"Dad, I don't know none of my friends have parties at this age so I would like not to have one either."

"Well, if you feel that way then we will not have one. Can I take you out to eat or is that out also?"

"No dad it is not. Yes, Dad you can I would like that."

"Good then no little girls party for my little girl."

"What do you want me to tell Bill about his mom?"

"Oh, nothing maybe I will see her at your ball game your first one is Friday night right."

"That is when the boys play."

"Well, are we not going anymore?"

"Dad, I have to go I am one of the cheer leaders unless I am playing that night which I don't believe we play on the same night anytime this year."

"Are the games at the same time as last year?"

"Yes, the freshman team plays at six thirty and the other game starts at about eight o-clock. I must be there for both games."

"Can I take you and stay for both games then?"

"Yes, if you want dad, I have to go study I have a major test in history coming up Friday and I need to do some tuft studying to prepare for it."

"Okay I was just making talk I seem to be starving for someone to talk to and I expect that to be you knowing you are really busy with all the in-school things going on so you go ahead I will just read a book."

"Dad I am sorry I miss our time together also, but this is a bad year I seem to have bitten off more than I can chew. Bill even asks me the other day if we were still friends, he never get to see me anymore."

"Well maybe just sometime, we need to just get away for a time and let God spend time in our live instead of letting the world take over what do you say."

"Okay dad, but I don't see that in my future from where I set right now."

"Well old dad we will figure something out to rescue us from this pit we seem to be in. So don't give up just yet."

"Okay while you enjoy the evening reading, I will work my reading into a good grade on this test."

Jody gives her dad a short peck on his cheek and goes to her study room leaving her dad to set and ponder just what has happened in their used to be fun life now with both, of them just a little bit unhappy with life in general. He had noticed that they had not had a good laugh together for a long time. He would ask Alice if Bill and she were going through the same symptoms and ask if she and Bill would go out to eat on Saturday evening. Maybe that would cheer Jody up and give her and Bill some time to catch up again. He decided he even needed something to help him. Friday night Tom took Jody to school one half hour before the game was to start. He set where he could see her and the main door not knowing if Alice would even come to the second game to see her son play. After the first game Tom went to the restroom and to get himself a soda. When coming back he noticed Alice was setting in his seat. So, he returned and got her a soda before returning to where he was setting.

"Hello Alice, it is nice to see you here I noticed you, so I got you a sprite is that okay."

"Well, I guess how are you is everything going okay?"

"Fine I have been thinking Jody and I have decided she was too old for birthday parties, so it has been canceled except I want to take you and Bill out to eat on Saturday evening. Jody tells me she has such a load at school that her and Bill never get to talk anymore, and I just thought it would give all of us some time to relax from the stress of everyday going hassles. If you want to if not I will understand I am just trying to change the drag in my daughter's life to release that smile that has been gone for a while. Thinking if I could get her away from this grind she might loosen up and start enjoying herself with her dad like we used to be."

"You make it sound so easy, maybe that is what both our kids need now. I well do it for Bill, but I will pay for ours you don't have to pay to feed us."

"I will not argue with you on that, but I still owe you for that dinner a long time ago."

"Good we will pick you both up at six o-clock Saturday evening."

"Is it a place of fancy, or just down to earth?"

"You can wear just what you have on, or something different but not dressy.

CHAPTER 10

Jody and Tom cleaned house and did laundry as usual. After lunch Jody said she was going to take a nap. Tom said.

"That will be grand but remember we should leave by five forty-five for dinner,"

"Dad, we don't have to go out for dinner, tonight, do we?"

"Yes, we do we have gotten out of our routine, and I think we will be in better moods if we get back doing some things together. We used to do all things and now with sports and school we are just going our separate ways and I get lonely all by myself. And I see you wanting to come home and be a hermit. Now I want us to be happy like we were even last year do you want to join me at doing something different."

Jody went by and kissed her dad on his cheek saying.

"If it will cheer you up and help me get from the cage, I am in I will go."

Jody went to her room and lying on her bed she kept thinking she wished Bill would ask her to do something they had grown apart or it sure seemed that way. She thought their friendship was still intact, but she wanted that special feeling more after as when she was just with him. She curled up with her pillow and next she knew there was knocking on her door.

"Yes, what is,"

And then she came too getting up to open the door.

"Oh, is there something wrong dad?"

"No but it is quarter to five you need to be getting ready to go. We don't want to miss our time slot, or we may wait a long time to eat."

"I will get ready what should I wear?"

"Just something that will make your loveliness stand out."

"Oh, we are going to a fancy place?"

"Well not that fancy but nice."

As they left home, they were chatting, and Jody was not paying attention as to which street they were going down until her dad slowed and turned into where Bill lived.

"Why are we stopping here?"

"Well, we owe these people a dinner and I have asked them to go with us so I could repay the debt. Is that okay with you?"

Jody felt heat rising in her face and neck. "Yes, daddy if you want it is okay with me."

"Well, I thought with Bill being your best friend besides me it would be okay for me to do this."

"Well, we have not talked much this year, so I guess he still is my friend."

"Good I will go tell them we are here be right back."

Tom went to the door and Bill opened it up looking past him towards the car.

"Are you ready if not we still have a little time no hurry."

Bill stepped out and Alice was standing there dressed up like a model waiting to walk down the aisle.

"Hello Alice wow you are stunning tonight I feel out of place, but I like what I see."

"Good evening, Tom we are ready as she shut and locked the door. Tom wanted to grab her, and his mind was racing with his heart pounding in his chest. What a beautiful lady and I get to go eat dinner with her. He had forgot that Bill and Jody were there. Without thinking he opened the door to let her in finding Jody setting there then he was without words. When Jody said.

"I am sorry dad I will get in the back seat."

As he closed Alice's door, he walked Jody around to let her into the back seat. He kept running this thought through his mind how am I going to get through this night. I have the most beautiful woman I have ever seen going to eat with me and as he got in the car the only thing he could think to say was.

"Are we all buckled up. Bill how have you been, and I think your game is getting better don't you think so mom."

"Yes, Bill and Jody are both doing great at their sports this year. Jody, I want to tell you I think you are the loveliest person. You are so polite on the court and with the other players. I just want to say also that you and your dad are close I can tell by the way you are when you are around him."

"Well thank you but you know I have had to raise and take care of this old man for a lot of years. Now I am glad some of it is sticking with him."

"Thank you, my young teacher does that mean, I get a star for satisfactory in class. Bill how have you been I have not seen you only on the field and court since we went fishing is everything going okay for you?"

"Yea as good as can be I guess mom keeps me busy most of the time."

"What he is saying we live a pretty sheltered live, but we must do that because of my job. I don't have a forty-hour workweek. My work comes in all hours of the day and night by fax. Each time I receive something I have only two hours to return it unless it comes in at night then I should return all them by nine thirty the next morning except on Sundays and that is when I do all my records and prepare my work sheets to fax back on Monday morning. That is how I get paid it has been heavy for the last six months and I have been giving Bill something to do to help me stay on top of my work."

"It sounds like a hectic life to me. I am glad I thought to ask you both to join us to give you a little break and so we can get to know more about both of you. How about some Saturday we go fishing again and have a picnic at the same time? What do you say Bill and you to Jody?"

That sounds great to me."

"Yea dad, sounds okay to me you need us women to watch over you like with food."

"Well let's set up something ahead of time so we can plan accordingly."

"Next week sounds good to me." Said Bill wanting to get out more.

"What do you say mom just one day of freedom from that house?"

"I can't do it next Saturday it is the end of the month, and I will be swamped. Can we do it in two weeks?"

"Sounds great now we have a date to plan towards, and now we are here and it is time to eat I believe that is why we can here. Last one in must pay."

Bill and Jody ran for the door with Alice on their heels while Tom was locking the car making him last, and that is what he wanted when he said it.

"You did that on purpose didn't you."

Said Alice as she turned to look at him. Tom was so engrossed in her eyes that he could not get words to come forth. Alice tapped him on his arm.

"Hello Mr. Bay, are you all right."

"Yes, I think so."

Knowing it was all he could do to not kiss those delicious lips he was looking at.

Then he placed his hands around her waist and kind of picked her up and put her behind him.

Then he turned her around to face him saying.

"Now you are last but not the least, and I will still pay."

CHAPTER 11

Two weeks went by in a hurry for Tom he could hardly wait to take Alice fishing and with Jody and Bill they could get reacquainted Saturday morning Jody asked.

"Dad why do you feel like including Bill and his mom in our time?"

"Is there something wrong that you are not telling me, or am I just imagining something that has you upset, or do you not want to go?"

"No, I was just asking."

"Well, it seems that I feel like I have a bad case of B. O. my daughter questioning me on what I subject, and Bill's mom does not seem to have anytime when I ask her and Bill to join us. Can you lighten my thoughts or am I just thinking wrong?"

"Dad don't jump to conclusions there is nothing wrong in what you did, but they are not our family, and I know you feel sorry for them because of the time they stay by themselves. I don't know why I get the cold shoulder when I ask Bill something about his life as if he would rather, I not know then he is standoffish for a while I have been thinking he does not like me anymore."

"How do you want him to like you? I thought you two were good friends."

"Well, we are I think I just can't put a finger on it so I just worry that I did something wrong."

"Well, I think if we just stay friends maybe it will ease up and then they will let us know what is bothering them, and what is such a secret will kind of fade away."

"I hope so because I really like Bill, he is the nicest boy in school and all the girls know it now, and I guess I feel like I might lose what I don't really have."

"Maybe they need more prayer do you know if Bill and his mom are Christians?"

"Bill says they are, but they don't go to church only on TV. at home. I don't see how they can enjoy it without some fellowship from other Christians like at church."

"Well maybe that is why we are in their lives. God has ways of bringing his children together in a place where he wants us to be. Now here we are I wonder if they are ready to go why don't you run up and see, and I will get the doors open and the trunk ready for Bill's tackle and rod."

"Hi Mr. Bay, is this going to be a good day for fishing I need to catch more this time. The last ones are all gone, and boy were they good eating. Just to let you know mom is just a little up and above when she must take something from others. She thinks everything is okay with the barter system if she is on the upper end of the giving. Me I say live and let live who is keeping count."

"That's a good way to look at it and you mother needs to change her mind, because Jody and I don't keep count either fair enough with you."

"Sounds great to me."

"Hi Mr. Bay, it is very nice for you and Jody to do this for Bill and me we owe you a lot for your friendship. Today I fixed our lunch and Bill said he was going to provide the meat and even cook it for us. He has become a good cook of course I am his biggest fan, and I just happen to think he is great. Maybe someday he will be some famous chef."

"Okay you all load up so we can get on the road. We don't want to be the last ones there we may not get a spot. Alice, you look very nice don't you think Jody?"

"Yes, dad she is, and has a way with clothes and besides she is a lovely woman."

"Thanks, you both but I just grabbed these old clothes and threw them on in between fixing lunch and finishing some work on my computer."

"Alice, you work too hard, don't you?"

"Yes, probably but someone must keep food on the table for this handsome guy that stays with me. Sometimes I wonder just where he puts it all."

Bill is saying nothing just setting and hoping his mom will slow down and not spell the beans.

"Jody how have you been it seems like we never get to see each other anymore. If it wasn't for your dad, we would be strangers."

"I am doing good too much school and trying to work in all the sports stuff. I have decided to give up volleyball this year it is too much. I am falling on my grades some, and dad and I never have anytime together anymore. I may give up cheer leading for the rest of the year also."

"Well, I wish you wouldn't do that you are the prettiest girl on the squad and the most enthusiastic. The guys and the team believe you keep up our moral with your leadership."

"Really do you really think that?"

"Well, you are my friend and yes I do believe that. I think with you just setting there makes me play better, and the others say the same thing."

"Well, I don't think I am that good and I know I am not that good looking."

"Jody as a spectator you are as Bill says, and you are a good leader and we think you are very pretty, then you let on it is not just the outside picture we see, but the enter soul that shines through. I believe that only a Christian would see you at your best. That is what we see, a very humble young lady that cares about anyone who would get close to you so you can help them. In the Bible, you would be a great severer of those around you."

"Thank you, Alice nobody has ever said anything, that nice to be before except my dad. You could be the mother I never had. I know how my dad feels but I don't know how others perceive me, course I am not looking for anyone to tell me so either. I am what God has made me and there are certain people I would like to show just what God could do with their lives. I know what he has done with mine."

"Hey! Said Bill we better get to the fishing hole before things get mushy in here. Tom what do you think?"

"It is nice when people open up and say their real feelings occasionally, we all tend to keep our thoughts to ourselves, but with Jesus he wants us to be friends to each other and that is what they are being as I hear them talking. Jody has not had an older woman to talk too all her life and I think Alice could do her a wonderful lot of good. Let's get these poles in the water you girls go get a place ready for lunch and we will bring the fish ready to cook."

"Mr. Bay what you said about Jody and my mom I think she needs someone to confide in like Jody for the last five years she has only me, and I don't need mothering that much, so I think it is good for them to be together. My mom does not understand me and my mom things she still wants me to be her little baby boy, and I don't know how to tell her I don't need that anymore without really hurting her. I am all she has for now and I don't know for how long. It is just all mixed up for us."

"What besides life itself is all mixed up is there anything I can do to help?"

"I would have to talk to mom before I can say much more, we have some issues that I cannot talk about anyway now."

"Do you and your mom know Jesus and what his power and love can do for you?"

"Yes, but for some reason he is so far away now, and we feel so alone."

With that tears came into Bill's eyes as he turned his head to keep Tom from seeing.

"Well son there are something that Jesus wants us to do for ourselves so we can be like a butterfly and squeeze out of our cocoon so we can fly. That time is the hardest to go through in his life and it is the same for us. Mostly because we believe we can do it all on our own."

"I believe you, but my mom has been hurt so much that I don't know if she has the strength for that squeeze in her life."

"What about your dad does he have any part in your life?"

"I don't know where he is and I don't think I even care. He hurt my mom so much that I believe I could really hurt him if he came around."

"I am so sorry Bill your mother seems to be the friendliest kind heartiest, loveliest woman I have ever meet in my life. I know from the way she shields her and you from any meaningful conversation about your past. Just between you and me I really like your mother and would like to take some of her burdens from her. I think she is a wonderful, beautiful lady that is caring much too much more than what God had intended for her to carry. I would really like to help you and her, but without your say so I am bound to stay out of your lives even though I know how much it hurts me and especially my daughter she cares about you more then she can let on. I would like for her to open up and let her true feelings out, but that has to come from Jesus and his timing and I believe that it will happen the same to you and your mother, I will just have to let the time arrive when Jesus thinks you all have the strength to handle it."
"Thanks, I like talking with you, but if we are going to be the bread winners as the meat people for lunch, we had better get these lines in the water."

Fifteen minutes later they had two large fish and were going to find the ladies for lunch.

"Mom look, what we got, nice hah."

"Yes, Bill you two did a great job I thought you had forgotten about lunch."

"Well, we have been just talking too."

"Probably more than fishing knowing you two."

"Bill let's get these fish cleaned and on the fire. We may have time to go and talk, I mean fish some more what do you think."

"Great where is the knife you want the heads on or off mom."

"Off I think this time I don't believe Jody and I want this to be some fancy restaurant today right Jody."

"Yes, no heads to be looking back at me."

As Bill comes back from the fire with fish on the platter he says.

"Okay I have done my part as is the rest of you did your part if so let's eat."

"Tom, would you bless this food and our time together."

"Yes, Alice I would be glad too. Dear Heavenly father I as your servant I want to thank you for this day and this time together with my daughter and our friends Alice and Bill may you look down on us and use your strength to fill our hearts with the fellowship you desire for us today. Thank you for the fish, Bill and I could catch, and may they also fill our bodies with your strength today. We ask all this in your son Jesus name. We love you Jesus A-men.

"And all Gods people said?'

"In a very low voice said Jody with a slight giggle."

"Come on Jody you know the answer I need to hear."

"Yes dad, and all Gods people said let's eat."

"Thank you."

CHAPTER 12

Jody and Bill saw very little of each other during the school time. Their basketball games schedule was different days and nights. Jody was being ground down by the hectic schedule she had. With playing and cheer leading with the boy's teams. Tom and Alice were spending Monday night with Jodie's team and Tuesday nights with Bill's team. Then again on Thursday, and Friday nights all over again. They saw very little of their children unless they were at the court or late at night when going to bed. Weekends everybody was crashed most of the time except when high school studying had to be done. Saturday nights were left open in case they wanted to go eat together which happened two or three times a month. Bill and Jody were beginning to bulk which left Tom and Alice alone. If they decided to go it was around Alice's workload. Tom thought sometimes he was getting the brush off not only from Alice and Bill but his own daughter. He had prayed about it and nothing seemed to change. He thought he would ask Alice to go on a scheduled, but every time he thought he would ask Alice seemed to get distant about certain things that came up. His daughter was always to tied up when he asked her. The only response was with Bill if he wanted to go fishing except he had to ask his mom if he could go. Tom tried reading some books to take away all the time he had for doing nothing, and his loneliness he could not get interested in the story. He put them all away and reached for his Bible to find that is the only time he had peace. On Saturday when Jody was sleeping he got on his knees and asked God to help him. "Dear Lord, I seem to need your help I am trying but nothing seems to be helping me in my dilemma. I am asking if you could help me to see or hear you guiding spirit. I thank you for all you have put into my life, but I am missing something that I cannot seem to find.

My life has been good, and soon in one and a half years my daughter will be going to college and I will be left here by myself wondering what and where you want me to be doing. I need you to help me get organized in my thoughts and start preparing myself for that, which is coming very soon. There are four people that seem to like each other but there is some dark shadow always coming between us how can I get these shadows to go away. I know we all love you and need an opening to start the human process, of opening, up to each other. I know my own daughter is hiding or sheltering something from me. I don't know how to comfort her without pushing her away. please take away my fears and losing her without knowing how to help her with that dark shadow that is hanging between us. Reveal to me what is or if I have done something to put that shadow in place. I don't want to, loose her to an unhappy circumstance that will separate us later in our short lives. If I am to help Alice and Bill then give me the strength and wisdom to do so on a loving way that they will not pull away from us. Help me to bring these burdens out so we can help and pray for your help to conquer these demands that leave us in the grip of Satan. I ask this today from my knees and my love for you. A-men."

Tom got up feeling like a big weight has been lifted from his shoulders. As he turned to go set on the porch he knew that it was his responsibility to start the process he had prayed about. He knew that God would give him the right words to say and what time to bring it up. Ah thank you Lord for your great kindness and power and for this warm sunshine flooding my soul, next he remembered was Jody shaking him from his shoulder saying.

"Dad can I talk to you or are you to sleepy."

"Sure, what time is it?"

"It is five o-clock you have been asleep for about two hours you must like this chair."

"Why as a matter of fact I do like this chair it has been with me or us since you were just a we little thing. Maybe I think about when you were just two years old. We used to set here almost every night all by ourselves. I have watched you sleeping on my lap for many long hours. What did you want to talk about?"

"Well I don't have a mom to talk to and there are things that I am not sure you can answer so I have been wondering if it would be alright with you if I would if you would care if I asked Alice if she could help me. I don't know what you think about her, and if I could use her for like a sounding board for my embarrassing thoughts that I need answered. If it is not okay then I guess I will have to call my mom, but I would rather not have her kind of input. What do you think I should do?"

"Is this why we have grown apart?"

"No I don't want to think of it as us growing apart it is I just don't know how to ask you without having our relationship as a father and daughter and maybe I am just too afraid to ask you. I have no way of knowing only by the way my friends talk and I don't want them to be my teacher if I can help it."

"Jody, I have no problem with you asking Alice these things. I have known this kind of things would come up soon or; latter and I would have stumbled through it and probably messed it up. You can ask Alice and see what she would say, and if you feel comfortable with her then you both have my prayers and blessings."

"Oh, daddy I have been thrashing this over for a long time, and not knowing just how to ask you. I am going to call her now and see if she would like to listen to me and help. Dad you do like Alice don't you I don't want this to ruin anything or start anything between you too."

"Yes, I like her a lot and, no you cannot hurt our friendship. There is nothing in my life or yours that would embarrass me in any way."

Jody is gone for ten minutes and comes back with a happy face.

"Dad Alice said she would be happy to help me. She is going to work out a time where we can spend thirty minutes at a time with her work and my school things."

"Well I will pray that she can help you with your womanly problems and between the two of you it will put a happy face back where it looks so good on you."

"Dad I am sorry it is not you I just feel like I need a woman to help me and Alice will not charge me anything, and now I will believe her in what she tells me more so than some stranger."

"Jody, I want you to believe in her and her help I think she needs someone in her life that can help her remove that dark shadow that is holding her back from enjoying life and the freedoms of life so she will ease up on Bill and he can shine like I believe he can."

"Dad you see things with them that keeps them from enjoying their life. You are so wise about these kinds of things and I trust you will be able to help them someday I know Alice needs more from life then what she is getting and because of that she is holding Bill back from his God given goals that could grow so good if he was not held inside the box he is in."

"Well maybe we can help both if we do as God is leading. If we pray for them every day God will use us to help if it is us that is to help them and Him to do the releasing of this thing that binds them up."

"Yes, I do and I am willing to help."

"Good let us pray that this is God's will for us and for Alice and Bill." "Heavenly Father my dad here on earth is the wise one and I believe what he says so if I am to be a part to help Alice and Bill get out of the box they are in then use me to do your will for them. Thank you that you gave me a good and wise father to raise me in a Christian home and guide me through life. Help me not to do the wrong things. I feel I need Alice and she may need me to spice up her life from the boring times she is going through I pray that we can become close. I thank you for our time together and that you will shower your blessings down upon us. Bless my dad I need him a lot. I have him and I love you so thanks from my heart. A-men."

CHAPTER 13

In two weeks of seeing Alice Jody had changed back to the wonderful girl her dad had known for so long she had more energy and was more involved in his life instead of spending all her time depressed in her room. She wanted to be friendlier with Bill, but he still stood back with his hands pushing away. Was he afraid to get close?

"Dad what would you say if I told you that I wanted Bill to be more than just my friend."

"I guess, I would say, that I need to get used to my little girl as being grown up. Why did you ask me and what did you want me to say?"

"I guess I wanted your approval that I could date him if he would ask me. Not that he ever will, but just in case I wanted to know how you feel. I never want to do something that would hurt you or the relationship that we have."

"Jody, I want you to know that I trust you in everything you do or take up. I know that you will do the right things whenever it arrives. You have my permission except you said if he ever asked you. Does that mean he does not know your true feelings about him?"

"I want to tell him, but we don't seem to be close anymore and I don't want him dating any other one because those girls don't want the same thing that I want for him. How do I tell him how I feel and get him to re-like me if he doesn't still do?"

"Well maybe you should ask Alice and see if see knows what he is thinking. She should more than likely tell you how or what he wants now. If that does not work then we can go fishing and I can get him to open up maybe."

"Would you do that?"

"Only if his mother would allow me to ask him, and her not telling you."

"Dad do you understand how I feel about Bill, or how I should feel about him?"

"I know how empty I felt when your mother pushed me away and I have lived with it for sixteen years. I know I can forget about how that left me so devastated because Alice has come into my life or our lives. Yes, I know how you feel, but you need to make sure it is what you want, and know that it is God's plan for you, or both of you. You still have time to figure that out."

"I don't want a used man dad, and I am so scared that my mother's life will come back and over ride in my life. I wouldn't want to hurt Bill like mom hurt you. Do you know how hard that is for me and whither I can turn my thoughts over to Bill about how I feel knowing he would run from me and I would lose him before I had, or felt his love for me."

"Yes, I know how you feel and that is some of my fear for Alice, but someday I have to talk to her to see whither we would ever have a chance to go farther in any kind of relationship."

"Dad we need to do something about this here we are setting here blabbering about our feelings and not knowing what to do about it. Maybe we need to go talk to Pastor Carl and maybe get some Godly advice, or answers to help us go forth."

"Maybe you are right maybe my praying is not enough maybe God wants us to leave our comfort zone and use some of our abilities instead of waiting for him to do all the work for us. Let's talk to Pastor Sunday morning to see if he has any time to work us in to his and our schedules."

"Dad are you prepared for what he might tell us whither to back away or pursue farther in our friendship and what if he wants to talk to them on the same level."

"Let's play like we are out of control and now God is back in control, and let him figure out the next move. I believe I would rather than be his choice then mine."

Sunday came and they asked to talk with Pastor Carl. He told them that his schedule was all used up for the next week and he would let them know when he could see them. When he called, he had Friday morning open but they could not make it because of school and work. he told them he does not see people on Saturday, but if they could meet him at one thirty he would make an exception. They agreed to be there and would not take up much of his time. When they arrived and told him their story he said I believe you need to pray that this is God's will for you and them? He would let you know some way if it is and if not then don't break the bubble or friendship and give it time. They agreed and left.

"Dad he did not know how to handle it did he."

"Well he is a young pastor and I am sure he has never been confronted with this kind of a problem yet but we will not give up on him or our friends. We are going to have a great friendship or no friendship at all. I do believe that they are ready to have someone caring about them. I do believe that Bill needs some fatherly advice and I know Alice has been hurt bad for some reason I do not know yet. I do know that she can be the sweetest kindest person I have ever meet. I wish I could get on the inside of that clear shield she has around her to see if I could help her."

"I feel the same way about Bill when I get to close he pulls away and when I am away I hurt and then he comes back. I want more than just occasional friend so I must make the decision to have him or not have him in my life even though I don't want to start over looking for a replacement. Because if he leaves I will be very hurt and may not want to get involved again with any male excluding my wonderful father."

"Let's not give up yet okay you know when the balloon breaks the air inside cannot be found, and I believe their balloons are getting very thin either they will come around or go away."

"Don't say go away dad I really like Alice and I trust her to help me and I wish her and Bill trusted us the same."

"Let's give it some more time as Christians we cannot do it without God and he will come around when it is time. We will he will give us the wisdom to notice when something is right or wrong and let us jump in to help."

"Dad you are older than I am you have more faith then I do, but I want to heal the sorrow that lives within our friends and I want the faith that Jesus will help us do this for him to free the spirits of our dear friends."

"Lord help my daughter and I to know that we are to help with the process of freeing the demands that have our friend's captive. Help us to free them to enjoy real life here instead of the shame of not knowing what you have for them to have joy in their hearts and your love in their souls. Help us to do what you expect us to do. Guide all our thoughts and word so as, to heal their souls and minds of their great dark shadow that has them. A-men."

"Okay now we just wait on Jesus to stand up with us. Then if it is okay then we can pursue or go somewhere else."

"Dad what if it is not what we want?"

"Jody my sweet girl we have just asked God to intervene for us so let Him do His work then we will know what to do. It will be revealed to us or will open the minds of our friends. Until then we wait for the Lord to do His part."

CHAPTER 14

"Dad I had a talk with Alice today, but we only talked about some of her issues. When I got there and she opened the door she started crying. She took quite a while before she could stop. She said she was so glad that I thought she was good enough for me to ask advice from. I believe that Jesus had spoken to her. She said she wanted to talk with you after my game if you knew where you could go so it would be quite."

"Why would that beautiful lady want to talk with me I wonder what she wants to talk about?"

"Dad I see love in your eyes and hear it in your voice when you talk about her. Don't get excited about anything yet until you find out what she has in mind."

"Oh, I wouldn't do that, that poor thing has a load built up inside her and I hope I am the one truck she wants to unload upon. Thank you, Jesus, for answering our prayers."

Tom picked Alice up for the game. They had the normal HI's how are you and Alice seemed to be more uncomfortable then she normally was. After the game, she asked Tom.

"Can we go somewhere quite so we can talk. You know I have been talking to Jody and things have come up that I want to discuss with you if it is okay."

"Sure, there is a small restaurant over the other side of town does Bill know you will be late?"

"I told him I wanted to discuss something with you so he is okay."

In the restaurant, they grab a back table and order coffee. All this time Alice has not said much only that she was excited about the game that Jody had.

"She seemed to be getting better each game I see her and I am liking it just to have her come over she is such a sweet girl. First I want to thank you for telling her to ask me. You know us girls have things that we cannot discuss with daddies. Not that they are bad, but personal."

"I am glad you two are getting it off she thinks you are the keenest woman she has ever known. You know she asked me that she had a choice either her mom or you and without question she picked you with my blessings."

Alice was holding her cup to her lips and saying nothing then the tears started flowing. She set the cup down and covered her face. Her sobbing was so strong that she was shaking. Tom touched her asking if she was okay, and if she wanted to leave.

"I thought I could do this without breaking down but is see I am not as strong as I thought I was. Yes, can we leave I can tell you in the car just as well. I don't want people thinking that you have hurt me."

Tom took her arm and guided her to the door throwing the waitress five dollars telling her to keep the change. Opening the door for Alice and holding her arm as she turned to enter the car she leaned into him and said.

"Could you hold me for just a little while to help me revive my strength."

Tom's heart was trying to get out of his chest as he placed both arms gently around her pressing her to his chest. What seemed like forever and still not long enough for Tom she pushed away and set down saying.

"I feel better now. Thanks, we can go now."

Tom crawled into his side and fastened his seat belt and started the engine.

"Is it okay if I just drive, that way I won't have to watch you and pay attention to the traffic."

"Yes, you can take me home now I think I am okay for tonight."

As he drove into her drive way he started to get out to let her go in, and she touched his arm and started crying again. Tom wanted to pull her to him and hold her for comfort, but he just set as she started talking.

"Tom I have to tell you something I cannot be your friend and keep this secret between us. First I want you to know I care a lot about you and Jody she is just like I always thought if I had, had a little girl of my own, and I know she would be just like Jody. Now brace yourself I think that I am in love with you and I can't tell you or show you unless I tell you of this bad thing that has put me here doing what I do. My name has not always been Day and I don't want to tell, or I can't tell you my real name and when I get through you will know why. Bill and I are here under the witness protection program of the federal government. My husband is spending the rest of his life in prison. Even though he opened his mind and brought a lot of people down and he is there because he would have no chance out here and I want to get us so far away from his actions as I can get and forget about my past and I believe you know how, or maybe that you can help me. You are so tender with me and I hope this will not change with what you know about me. I thought we had a good life until that day when the F. B. I. knocked on my door and took him away. I have not seen him since and now I don't want too. That same day they came and took Bill and I away I have very little of our things from the past they went through and took everything from our past. They took everything and burned it giving us a new identification and put us through I don't remember how many places with guards twenty-four hours a day until just a month ago. Then they finally told us we were clear of any trouble, but they left a phone number if we needed any help. I want a new life and I am scared to death still. I really like being around you and Jody and I know in time Bill can forget all this with some help. I don't want you to say anything to night but I want you to think about what I have just told you and keep it to yourself for the time being. Now I think I had better go in."

Tom got out of the car to open Alice's door for her to get out. He helped her out and closed the door to shut out the light from the car. Then, looking down into her eyes, he put his hands upon her waist and said.

"Alice I am going to kiss you and I want you to hold still and just relax is that okay with you."

She could not say a word even though her heart was pounding and her thoughts were why would he want to kiss me after putting him through the bad time in her life. Tom gently placed his lips upon hers and without any pressure he held that kiss for a ten count then released her and walked her to her door.

"Thank you for, when you were holding me tonight I knew it would be that way."

"Good night Alice and as you said I think I am in love with you so I feel the same way and I want to hold you longer, but I don't want to scare you away. See you tomorrow night at Bill's game do you want me to pick you up."

"Do you really want to if so I would appreciate it very much."

As she turned and threw her arms around his neck and kissed him rather hard then returned to do the same thing again. "I had better go before I think about waking up from this dream."

"Please believe me this is no dream I want to go home with you, but I know I can't do that now, but I want you to know just how you have been affecting me."

"Alice, it has been good to hear you open up to me it is and will always be a secret for you and Bill. Your, want is my desire and in God's timing. Until tomorrow evening well; and now know that I care about you and Bill. Jody is so happy now I can't believe how she has grown in just two week with you again, and God's timing. I want to kiss you again to say goodnight, but that means I don't want to go so just goodnight."

"Tom please do not hold my past against me. I want you to know I had no choice, and Bill and I are victims of an ungodly Act and the evil one is the fault. Please care for me the same as before you knew about it."

"As for now, and on in the future you have that love from me."

The next morning Tom was cleaned up, dressed up, tidied up, and tied up he could not get to Alice's place fast enough. He wanted to make sure that she was as real as he projected her in his mind. He wanted to hold her until she would never cry again for the past in her life. He wanted those kisses to never stop, oh how he had missed the touch of a woman who thought he was something special. As he stood by the door waiting for Alice to open it he could not stop thinking could she be the one God has had him waiting for so long. When the door opened there stood his dream shinning in its entire splendor. With such a lovely smile and those lips that were made for kissing eyes that he wanted to go into to see if all behind was as real as he thought in his mind.

"Hello, you lovely creation of God how nice just to look upon you a dream come true."

"Hello, are you the man I was with last night. If you are then why am I waiting to be hugged and kissed until my legs will not hold me up."

"Will it matter if I do this in the door way or inside the house of the most beautiful lady I have ever met. Oh, never mind."

As he pulled her to him in the embrace of two people who had missed this kind of attention for so long. After a while of about five minutes he backed up, and said.

"Do you want the neighbors to start talking?"

"Right now, I do not care if they do or not. I am kissing someone I have been waiting for so long. Now you can tell me why you stopped was it to see me about something?"

"Yes, I did not want this dream to stop. If it is true do we tell the kids or just do our thing?"

"Bill and I do not keep secrets, and I want everyone to know about you."

CHAPTER 15

Jody and Alice were meeting more often than there two times a week. Jody did not know about Alice and Bill's past, but she was getting what she had missed for so long. The loving care of an older woman who cared about her and her life.

"Alice!"

"Yes!"

"I want to ask you something it is the way I feel about you. I want you to know how much I appreciate what you are doing by talking the time to spend with me. I really care about you, and I love the way you treat me as if I was your daughter, and I want to know if you can be my secret mom?"

"Jody, oh girl."

And with tears in her eyes, she goes and wraps her arms around Jody, and with praise and thanks giving she thanks God for this special time.

"Jody, thank you, you have opened a new hidden place of my life and I will be happy, glad, excited and honored to be your mom and it does not have to be kept a secret. Let the world know after all these years I have my little girl. Oh, Jody you and your dad makes me so happy something that I have not felt for so long. Oh praise God for answering my prayers."

"Thank you, mom, but what about, what will dad think?"

"Jody, can you talk about your mom and what that part of your life means to you?"

"As you know I have a mom like everybody does, but I have no recollection of who she is and I don't feel now I want to know. She has been at my home one time in the last seven years I did not like what I saw then, and that ended her in my life at that time. Only

God will heal that hurt in my life and I believe that he has sent you as my true mom."

"Jody if you told your dad what, do you think he would say?"

"I don't know I just don't want him to think I don't need him anymore. He is my whole life, and I will never love anybody like I love him."

"I take it your mother as far as you can remember was not a nice person did she hurt you in anyway mentally or physically that you can remember?"

"Mostly physically and most of that was the way she treated my dad he just took it until she started on me when I was about, I think ten years old. I can still see the hurt on my dad's face when he came from her room after telling her to go home to her folks and not come back until she could become the woman he had married. She will never be back and if so he will never take her back."

"Are they still married or divorced?"

"I do not ask I don't want to see the look that will come to his face if you want to know you will have to ask him."

"Jody just between you and me I want to tell you a small secret. I have a past with Bill that I have told your dad about it. It has been very hard for me the last few years. I want you to know that I am very much in love with your dad. If something happens while I want very much and only with God's blessings for all of us to be together. What would you say if I was to become your stepmom?"

"Oh! No! Oh! Oh! Yes. Do you think it could happen oh I am so excited I am going to cry?"

As the tears came forth and they wrapped their arms around each other with the sobs and crying got louder until Bill stepped into the room to see what was happening.

"Ah um is there something I need to know mom what is going on?"

"Oh, Bill I am so happy Jody wants me to be her mom and I have accepted what do you think?"

"Whatever just don't go overboard."

And then he walked back through the door.

"Well, he didn't seem very happy or excited about that. I wish I knew why we were not close friends like we started out to be."

"Jody Bill and I must someday tell you about our prior life. Somehow, I feel your dad and I must understand as much as we can to be able to bring you two into that pain to be released, I don't want you to worry about it, it is coming soon I need to talk to Bill about it first to see how he feels. Can you forgive me for that length of time?"

Mom I am so happy that you want me it has nothing to do with your past I just want us to have a future. If dad and Bill is part of it then so be it. That would make it that much better."

"Okay lets us be us and then we can let the two men decide if they want us for who we are how about that."

"Mom, do you think my dad has let's say eyes for you as you do him?"

"Well, when I told him about my past and when I was crying, he held me and kissed me good night. I don't know what that meant yet I must give him some time to sort out what I told him. If he can that is good if he can't then I lost what I did not have but I got that dark shadow off my back and out of my mind and my life with him, and I feel great that I finally had the nerve to let it go. I emptied the bag and now I will deal with whatever comes from it."

"My dad kissed you?"

"Yes, and I liked it. Yes, and I want more of the same as soon as I can get it to happen."

"Wow! I have never been kissed by anyone but my dad. Can you tell me is it much different when someone else kisses you? You know like on the lips."

"Oh, yes you wait, and you will see."

CHAPTER 16

With ball games on Wednesday and Thursday, and Friday nights they never talked much about Alice's confession of her troubles. When they left the Friday night game Tom asked if she was hungry or wanted to talk.

"I am not hungry, but we can talk I would like that."

As she slid closer towards him and put his arm around her neck

"Would you like to go watch the stars at the beach it looks like a good night it is very clear."

"Oh, that sounds like too far I have a busy day tomorrow I get behind with all the games we go to, but I want to go to the games. I what, I want is to just be close to you if nothing else just, to be able to touch your hand. Do you have something special or specific you want to talk about?"

"Yes, as a matter of fact I need to know what you think of me as a friend and a man. I have something I want to talk about, but I really need your input as what you think of me."

"Well, Tom, I find you very attractive, very pleasant to be around. I like your soft even voice, I like your car, I like you to hole me and I want you to kiss me. I don't care where or how much money you have. I think you are one supper great father. I like your smile and if you would kiss me I would shut up."

"Why should I kiss you I am enjoying what you think of me except one thing."

"What is that, that I ran out of thoughts?"

"I want to know if you could or would like to stay with me for the rest of my life. I am asking you if you are available to be my wife."

Alice could not make the words come from her mouth they seemed to be lodged in her throat. After coughing she started to talk, but Tom interrupted her asking.

"Did I do something wrong if so you do not have to answer me until you feel up to it. I am sorry if I startled you."

"Oh Tom."

And the tears started flowing down her cheeks and she was sobbing too much to make any sound.

"Tom got out and went to her door to help her out so she could get some air.

"Tom as she leaned into his chest do you really want me that much. I really don't know what to say, only since you asked not even you can stop me from loving my husband to be."

Throwing her arms around his neck and they held their kiss for a long time finally Tom said.

"Hear in this school parking lot and in from of God and any other one watching I accept your answer to be my wife. When or how fast can it happen?"

"Can we do it tonight?"

"Yes, but where?"

"I guess it is a little soon we will have to prepare for it and we do need to let the kids know that they are going to be part of the same family."

"We had better go before they ask us to leave I have to get home, but I really don't want you to go can we tell Bill tonight or do you want to tell them when we are all together."

"How about dinner tomorrow night?"

"Good I will fix and you and Jody can come to my house."

"No, we will go out it is going to be on me."

"Tom!"

"Yes!"

"I love you more than anything I have ever known can't tell you how happy and full of joy just to be standing here besides you."

"Well, what are you thinking right now?"

"Really you don't want to know do you?"

"Then I will tell you what I want to do."

"Good!"

As she stood on her tip toes and placed another kiss on his warm lips and then asked.

"Well tell me."

"I want to hole you laying in our bed naked with nothing but skin touching what would say to that?"

"I say my knees are turning into noodles and if you don't take me home I may try undressing right here. Oh, Tom we sound like little teenagers wanting but knowing it is not right. What would Jesus say if he was here?"

"He is here that is why we are not doing it, but it is okay to talk about it so we can have that time on that special night."

"You had better take me home I forgot I have work to do and I hope I can unwind so as not to make too many mistakes."

As Alice returned to the car seat Bill came up leaving for home asking.

"Do you to have trouble you are still here or does Jody need a ride home?"

"No, we were just enjoying the night air and talking you had a great game tonight what was it twenty-two points you are getting too good for the rest of the team."

"I am being constantly told by the coaches that I need to let some of the other guy shoot some, but they keep feeding me the ball even if I give it back they are afraid they will miss. So, I just keep shooting."

"Anyway, I wanted to tell you that I thought you are one great basketball player."

"Thanks Tom see you later. Mom I am going to get a hamburger with the guys."

"Okay you be careful, and I will see you at home later."

"He is a good kid you have done a great job of raising him."

"Tom, he has been sheltered for so long and now I want to trust him by telling him that the past is over, and he can start a new life except he cannot talk about all the hidden things. He sometimes gets depressed because he has no friends that he can confide in and cannot mention anything about his past or his dad or any of his relation. All he knows is he and I and keep quite don't say anything keep away from people unless mom is right there with you. Now I am going to tell him he can start life at the grand old age of seventeen years of age. Just like he was born yesterday as big and as smart as he is without knowing how he got where he is at."

"I understand, but we will have to be careful to see if he can except all this and help guide him through this so-called new life he will be thrown into. I know that we can do that, and I believe he is strong enough to handle it if we don't just give it all to him to handle by himself. I want you and him to know that you needed a daughter and you found one. I needed a son and I want Bill to be that son for me. He looks all grown up but still has a lot of growing up to do before he can understand all that has happened in his life and why it all happened."

"Tom I still need to get home, or I will not be able to go tomorrow night I am sorry I wish this night never had, to end, but it has to for my sake and ours I am sorry."

"Please do not use that word it is not good, and I have a problem with it. Think of it like this people should not say and do things that they have to constantly have to apologize for saying or doing it,"

"What should I say then?"

"You already said it you had to get home, and it is my responsibility to honor that request."

"Boy, am I going to have to catch up and I want to honor you and, also honor our Lord Jesus as well. Tom I can only say how much I have fell in love with you. Goodnight until I see you again."

"One other thing, don't tell me goodbye that means you don't want me around, and I know someday you will say it, and I hope you don't mean it."

"If I ever do I want you to hug and kiss me back into your arms and life. We are going to grow together and become old and happy."

"Tom please leave before I cannot let you go. Do not kiss me anymore, or you will have to be what you might say ruff to me. I want you to not go and yet I know you have to for our sake and be honoring to God."

CHAPTER 17

Saturday evening Tom and Jody went to pick up Alice and Bill. As they were eating, they talked about the ballgames and how school was going Bill was having some trouble in a couple of his subjects. Alice was being swamped with hospital work and having trouble trying to think of how to tell Bill. During desert time Tom decided it was time to change the subject and talk about what had transpired between he and Alice.

"Jody, you know how much I care and love you, and Bill I have grown fond of you in the last six months to a year. I have something to tell you and I want your attention and understand that you listen."

With this he took a ring box from his pocket and opened it up.

"Alice, we have talked about this and now I think it is time to let the kids know how we feel. I give you this ring as a token of how I feel about you. Kids I have asked Alice to be my wife and she has consented to do so. Don't say anything yet there are some issues that have to be addressed and we want you two, to want the same things we want."

Jody jumped up and went to Alice and gave her a big hug and with tears running down her cheeks she told her dad thanks as she gave him a hug and kiss on his cheek. Bill set there as if not knowing just what to say until his mother ask him.

"Bill, we want you to be excited about this also can you tell us how you feel about changing our lives?"

"I don't know what to say only if that is what you two want then I cannot stop you. But anyway, I now am going to have a sister that I should change my mind about. I mean she cannot just be a friend anymore. I can beat up on her if I want and she will have to like it.

I don't know how to treat a sister since we are the same age we could be twins or whatever."

"Bill I am sure my daughter will not stand still and let you beat her up and we hope it does not come to that."

"I mean I can't be jealous of her if some other boy wants to take her on a date, but I guess I could go with them. Jody, I don't know what we will do but I think we need to set down and talk about this don't you?"

"Bill, I think you will make a great brother and I could be jealous of you with some other girl so we might have to double date all the time."

Tom turns to Alice saying.

"Sounds just like what brothers and sisters should sound like what do you think?"

"Well as a mother I will be very upset if all you two do is fight. Now I must be a party! You know what, but I have my work to get done and Bill you need to help me. This is just the start of what I have dreamed about for so long. I want a happy family that loves each other and wants to make it work as much as I do."

"Jody, can we talk tomorrow afternoon that is if I have some free time from my workload that I would rather not do on Sunday, but why change after so many years."

"Where would you like to talk your house or mine and what time."

"Two o-clock at your house if it is okay with your dad."

"Kids you can talk wherever you need too. I will probably be taking my usual nap."

"Bill if we get enough done tonight then you can have the time. I know you both need to access each other's minds about this sudden surprise that has entered your thoughts. We want you to be able to ask and get all the information you need. Tom and I have had our thoughts, and we have both agreed to them and open to you both for your input. Jody and I have gotten to know each other quite well in the last month. I would like Tom and Bill to do the same if possible."

"I believe we can don't you think so Bill we can and will have time to spend fishing and whatever. Oh, and for something all of us to think about as I have been thinking. I would like with our entire blessings together look for a new place to live. I even thought about a small place out in the country ten acres or so, some place close so you both could finish school here."

"Mom, I like that and I am ready when do we start looking?"

"Well, it depends on how soon we become a family."

"Let's start now what do you think Jody a place out in the country clean air and no neighbors looking in your windows."

"I don't know I am kind of a city girl."

"Well, the three of us can change that, well maybe we need to talk a little more about that tomorrow."

'Before we go, I need to place this ring on your finger."

They said their good nights and Tom and Jody drove home.

"Dad have I ever told you that you are a great dad and if I had to pick a man, I would have picked someone just like Alice we are going to have so much fun together."

"I am glad I hope Bill feels the same about me. All though you two have a head start on us, but you are more outgoing than Bill is so it may take us some time to get where you two are."

"Dad, I don't know if I can go to sleep I am so excited what a day."

As she gave him her usual hug only a little bit harder and his favorite cheek kiss.

"Dad if you want to live in the country then I will like it also. I just said that to get Bill's goat. So, let him figure it out okay."

"Okay dear daughter goodnight."

Tom and Jody both lay for a long time until sleep finally overcame them. Sunday school and church were the same until someone saw the ring on Alice's finger, and before long the whole church knew about the wedding. Even the Pastor had his thoughts input.

"Who is going to be the lucky man to perform this marriage between you too?"

"Whoever has the first open date in the next month."

Said Alice with a smile which lite up her whole face.

"For you two I am free when you are ready."

"It will be something small and no presents from anyone we just want to go on as if nothing has changed."

"Okay Tom you name the day, and I will be ready. Alice what do you want."

"I want to spend from now on enjoying this very handsome man and my new daughter. We are the wedding party unless you say we need more."

I need a witness beside the family, and my wife can do that. You two get your paperwork done and let me know."

At two o-clock Bill rings Jody's doorbell. When she opens the door, he is staring at his new sister with other things on his mind. "Well come on in it is me you don't have to stare. Just say hi Jody nice to see you. You look refreshing can we talk ha, ha. Come on in we can have the den so as not to disturb dad and his nap. Would you like some water or a soda I can get yours while I get mine? Here make yourself at home be comfortable I will not be long."

Bill sets in a love seat coach and just looks around not knowing how to start this talk that he wanted to have with Jody. When Jody comes back she hands Bill his drink and sets down right beside him. As Bill kind of scoots to the arm and Jody does the same to touch him saying.

"Bill, we can do this we are brother and sister but it, it is going to make you feel uncomfortable I will not set so close. It's okay I guess but what I need to say I would rather you set facing me. So, my neck does not get a kink in it."

"Well okay if that is the way you want it, I just wanted to be close to you to see how it would feel."

Jody jumps up and leans to kiss his forehead and sets down across the room and curls up in the chair.

"Okay brother what did I do that you want to talk to me."

"Jody come on you did nothing, but I only wanted to know how you felt about my mom and your dad and us being siblings like overnight. I mean how am I supposed to feel about you and now get used to have a man figure in my life. I know you and your dad are close and now you and my mom are getting close. I am wondering how and what you thought about us. I mean can we still be friends and brother and sister all at the same time. Do you see any problem with us being in the same house and eating at the same table?"

"Are you telling me that you care about me above just being a friend."

"Well, I do like you and I have thoughts about you, and I would like to. Oh, I don't know how I feel about this, and I know you can help me if I blow something with your dad."

"What are you talking about what do you want me to help you with."

"Bill, I want you to be my brother and I want you to accept me as your sister and I am a loving person I may want to hug and kiss you goodnight just like I do my dad and your mom. Is that what you are afraid of if so then tell me not to do it. Bill, I love being around you and I would be upset if you dated another girl, but I need this relationship with you to make me a whole person I have not had this to know how I would feel and I am excited about it. Bill, I said I love you and I want you to be a good brother because I need it and I hope you need it too. I didn't say I was in love with you even though sometimes I want to do silly things that I cannot do. This will make me more aware of how I feel towards you. I don't know how you feel about me you have never opened and let me know. I have let my feelings go just so we could be friends and I want the same things now that you are going to be my brother friend. Tell me now how you feel about me."

"Jody for a long time now because of our living conditions that you do not know about yet. I have these strange feelings that come and go when I am near you, I like what I feel but I do not know what to do about them."

"What do you feel, can you tell me, or do I just guess?"

As Jody gets up and goes over and sets on his lap and puts her arms around him.

"Is this what you feel or is it something else."

As she gets up and goes back to her chair.

"Did you like that what I just did you feel good or bad about it."

"Good and that is about what I am talking about how am I going to deal with it now being around you so much."

"Bill I will not let you upset me or I will not do anything to hurt you if you love me then I say wow I want you to love me I want you to think I am the only one for you and some day if you want to marry me I will say yes, but we are only seventeen and we have a lot of living to do before that could happen. Now tell me I am right so I can get my feeling under control also. Come on I am your sister am I right or not."

"Yes, Jody you are right, but I will still have a hard time of it."

"Bet you won't."

"What do you mean by that?"

"What I am saying is like white on rice. When I have the urge to talk to you I do not have to wait until I see you at the ball games or in school. I just get to come and open your door and walk in."

"But you cannot do that, what if I am undressed and in bed?"

"That will be the fun part."

CHAPTER 18

Tom and Alice told the kids they needed to talk to them a while after Sunday evening service. They were all setting in Alice's living room when Tom said.

"What Alice wants to tell or talk about I already know and I am okay with it and Jody I want you and Bill to understand we are going to make this work. No matter what's thrown at us okay Alice I will let you tell them."

"Jody, I want you to listen while I talk to Bill and by then I think you will understand. Okay Bill Tom knows all about our life of living in fear of something your dad drug us through years ago I want you to know that the people that has been protecting us are no longer out there. I am not sure we are out of the woods yet but I feel better about it. I have never liked the way we have had to live and hide all the time never going or doing things other people did. I want you to know that we are freer now than ever we can start over. You can have a dad figure in your life and I can have a daughter in mine. I want you to love your sister as if you had known her all your life. I want you and I to have fun and peace for a change. I want you to know what a real home would, could be like where we can go in and out our doors without looking before we do. I want you to know you can have friends and do the things other boys get to do with their families. I want you to be as excited about this as I am. I want you to know what it would have been like to have a sister to have fun with, and yes even fight with occasionally. I cannot give you all the last years back, but I want and with Tom's help you to be able to go and do and open to others. I believe that when you do this you are going to be as happy as I am. I am with Tom I will live where he puts me I love him that much. You said let's go look now; yes, I am ready to look also. I want this house that has held us captive for about two years out of my life and I hope and see you feel that same way. Bill before you are an old man I want you to feel that you can be happy too. Do you understand what I am telling or asking you to do? Jody, do you understand what I am saying because you are one big reason and you can help me do the things to help Bill feel more at home. I see how you feel about each other and I know this is going to work in our favor. Bill, do you have any questions."

"No mom I am okay and you know I have only one person that I have ever really loved and that is you and I know I can do the same towards Jody and my new dad. If it is okay to call you that?"

"Son I would not have it any other way and I would be honored for you to call me dad. I think that in time there will be times that we do not see eye to eye but that is to be expected of two adults. I think you know that I am a very fair person. Jody how do you feel about this?"

"Dad I love this guy he has been like my brother for a long time a least as long as I have known him. I am going to shower him with sisterly love until he has caught up for all the time he never had me."

Jody goes over and tells Bill to stand up and when he does she throws her arms around his neck and give him a big hug and a soft kiss on his cheek saying.

"Now how do you like your sister now I could have bitten you but I could have done that anytime."

Bill with his red face just stands there not knowing what to say.

"I see we have the making of a good family having lots of fun. Son get used to her she likes to embarrass me sometimes too. That is just the way she is when she can be so to speak loose with people she loves. Now tomorrow I am going to see some realist state people and see what they have or what we can look at. We need a two-bedroom home with a two-car garage."

"Dad what do you mean a two-bedroom home I am too old to sleep with him, and I want my own room."

"You know what I have to look for is a four-bedroom house it will be the first time I ever lived in more than a two-bedroom house. See how this is working and everyone should make some change.

Okay then we need a den or office for Alice to do her work in and a big two-woman kitchen with a large porch for Bill and me to set and talk on. Now we need to go to bed you got school tomorrow. I hope by next Saturday we will have some places to look at. Good night family."

The week went well everyone was still talking about their new family Tom and Alice got the paper work done. Saturday morning, they were to be married at ten o-clock. Just before Tom and Jody left for the church the realest state agency called and ask if they had time to look at a couple of places. He was told they would be home waiting for him but it would be around one o-clock. He would pick them up there would be four people. At ten the Pastor signed his papers and told them they could not back out now. They said their vows with Jody and Bill standing up with them. After fifteen minutes, it was over and the Pastor had to have time for prayer. They left the church and Tom said they all had to come in his car.

"What will we do with our car?" asked Bill.

"Just leave it in the parking here at the church for now we have to go look at some property as soon as we can go home and change into some different clothes".

"Wow!"

Said Bill.

"This family does things in a hurry so let's go. Hey sis I get the right back seat."

"Not if I get there first."

"Tom I think our kids are going to be fun don't you they are so much looser now then any time I can remember."

"I praise God every day that He brought us all together through our kids. They needed more in their lives and Gods knows, and I believe that is why they became such good friends, and I am very thankful that Tom had such a sweet, nice, wonderful, lovely mother."

"Please do not flatter me. We still must find time to; well you know. "

"No what do we still have to do?"

"We have to get used to sleeping in the same bed, and what goes with it."

"Are you telling me we have to have sex."

"Wow! Now I am getting nervous, I want you to know that I sleep all over the whole bed."

"Oh, I like that it means you are going to be all over me all night long."

"Yes, I can hardly wait, by me we could go now and look for a house in a month or two."

"We may be all wore out by then."

"Yes, this family is going to be fun for a change."

CHAPTER 19

They hurried home and the realtor was waiting for them. They climbed into his van and were off. The first place was too close to town and there was a neighbor that was forty yards from the house. The second one was a nice place, but there was eighty acres to the farm.

"Too much we only want ten acres no more."

"Well, this next place is kind of a, well you will see it I think you may like it, it has about fourteen acres with a large pond for fishing. It is not a new place, but a well taken care of place. I believe it is twelve years old. It has an outbuilding that is twenty-four by forty. It has a wraparound porch on three sides. It has three bedrooms upstairs and one down. One bath up and one-half bath plus the master bathroom down. The only block to this house is that they are waiting for their home to be finished before they can move. It is just up the road be there in one minute or less."

"Is there fish in the pond."

Asked Bill.

"It says fishing pond, so I believe that means fish in the pond. Here we are it is nice because it set back off the road a way and up a small rise."

"Oh, Tom this is a beautiful home oh I can't wait to see inside."

"Okay everyone out."

They toured the outside and the pole barn and the outlaying grounds. Bill and Tom went to survey the pond and the pastureland. Jody and Alice walked around the yard and house to get some idea of the planting of flowers.

"Well mom what do you think?"

"Jody, I can't believe this it is such a peaceful place oh I really like it, do you?"

"Yes, I get the bedroom on the right so the sun will wake me in the morning."

"You got it well that is if we get this place with your dad's blessings."

"They won't care mom they will have a place to go fishing."

When they all got in the van Tom asked what the price was.

"Sounds like we may have a deal. We have two houses in town, and I know one is for sale and they can move right in as soon as we clean up and move out. The other one I was thinking it may be a good rental place, but for now this is the day that this family just got married and we need to go home and decide this later can you come by this evening. We will show you the one we will sell."

Tom and Alice told the kids we are going to be gone until Sunday evening and you can stay at home and watch the places, I am sure you can find something to do like sorting things you want to keep and the rest you want to get rid of.

"Bill, we will drop you off at the church to get your van. Bill, will you go in the morning to get Jody for church."

"I guess I could, but she had better be extra nice or I will."

"Hey brother you are going to eat here for lunch so you had better be good yourself or I may mix something from the neighbor's yard in your sandwich."

"Come on mom I think they both have enough fight to take care of themselves for at least twenty-four hours."

After dropping Bill off to get the van Tom and Alice spent the night and day in Mobile. They enjoyed each other and reliving for the first time in a long time. They discussed their future and thanked God for the present. They made a pact to bury the past because they didn't want it dictating how they went each day. They prayed for their children and their lives together that the Holy presence of God would replace the evil things that they had lived with. They had a dream for how they were to live their lives in supporting Jody and Bill and doing whatever God brought into their paths. They decided to rid their lives of all things even those which they now owned and restart their lives a new under the love and kindness of

Jesus Christ their Lord and Savior. They arrived home to a house that all could not live in and that dedicate their future and the decision to act accordingly. They did not want to be separated nor separated from their children. Alice's house had three bedrooms or Bill could sleep on the coach in Tom's house. On the way home, they made the decision that Bill would sleep in the bedroom and Alice would still work at her house until they could purchase the house they liked. At home, they stopped at Alice's house and got some clothes and Bill decided he could sleep on the coach for a short time. They arrived at Tom's house and told Jody of their decision. Her first response was.

"Whoopee I could set on my brother's bed and make him like it."

She got a pillow in the face from her brother. They told Bill and Jody of their decision about now passions, and they had to make their own decision about what they wanted to keep and what they wanted to throw away. The good stuff they would put in one place and when it was all there, they would have an auction to get rid of it. When they had the new home, they all would go and pick out the new furniture for each room they were now in the process of being a real family. Jody asked her dad.

"Why get rid of all our stuff and go buy all new?"

"Because we made a pack that we are going to start all new and take no old baggage with us to leave the past behind us and be easier to forget about it. Each one of us has certain personal things that mean a lot to just us that we all can keep if it is something that we cannot live without, but remember the past is dying and the future is bright so let's let our light shine for all to see. Between ballgames and work they started the clean-up of their old lives putting it in boxes and storing them in Tom's garage and he parked outside. They removed the coach and put Bills bed in the living room. They were happy and crowed, but they were having fun separating themselves from the bondage of the past. Each night they held hands, and all prayed for the transformation of God's grace and love to help them into the future and to become a real family. They wanted or needed God to act in their new home. After three weeks Tom was called to sign the papers. Alice had her house put on the market with the understanding she needed it until they had their new place so she could move her office belongings. She had to do her in homework every day. They moved all her big furniture into her garage and clean up the whole house. The office room was all that was intact. It became a lonely place to spend all day, but she knew it was devil trying to discourage her. Most of her and Bills clothes were in boxes at Tom's house. Jody's room was where all the boxes were stacked that they all wanted to keep. She was now being in a storage unit she could not even make her bed from only one side. Her and Bill did there studying at the kitchen table. They all fought over the bathroom. They were happy yet they were getting up set a lot because of the upheaval in their lives. It had been six weeks like this Bill and Jody were both through with basketball and that put them in a little more crowed home more hours than they could partake and be happy in. the phone rang one evening and Jody said.

"Hello this is the Bay home may I help you?"

"I am calling to tell Mr. Bay the house will be ready to move into by this weekend sometime Saturday afternoon. Would you let your family know?"

"Yes, thank you."

She hangs up the phone and ran to the living room and was bounding on Bill's bed when he came from the outside asking why she was tearing up his bed. She through the covers off onto the floor and was dancing around when he grabbed her and threw her onto the bed and pinning her there.

"What is wrong with you? Why did you mess up my bed?"

"Because I just heard some good news for a change when the phone rang."

"Like what?"

She through her arms around his neck and kissed him for the first time saying.

"We get to move starting next Saturday or Sunday, and I am so happy I just felt like messing up this dump we are living in. I can't wait until mom and dad get home."

"Well, here they are."

As the front door opened with, a start and a gasp from Alice.

"What happened here?"

"Dad, mom I just received a phone call, and we get to move to our house this weekend and I was just celebrating early."

They all grabbed hands and was dancing around in a circle when there came a voice from the open-door way.

"Hello, am I interrupting something."

It was the realtor.

"Oh, no this is the way we act our normal way of greeting each other at the end of the day. What would you like or what do you have for us."

"I called about your new house, and I have some information on Alice's house and to tell you Friday afternoon we must close on the house you are buying. I have and offer, and it is close to your price if you want to except it."

Tom and Alice looked at the figure and she said where do I sign."

After signing he told them.

"The new people need to move as soon as they can, and we can close on your house on Friday after closing on the other house if that is okay with you."

Alice looked at Tom and then said.

"Okay but I will need to move my office I still have work to do and reset the office at our new home."

"Fine see you all Friday afternoon at the land and title company downtown on Main Street. Oh, and go ahead and tear up, you deserve it goodnight."

Jody jumped upon Bill's bed and then again, she jumped and something broke letting the mattress fall with her falling to the floor.

"Now you did it little sister you broke my bed and now I will be sleeping in your bed and you can sleep on the floor."

Jody got on her knees in front of Bill and was crying.

"Bill I am sorry I just got carried away please forgive me."

Bill places his hands on each side of her face and lifted her up saying.

"Just because you are now my sister. I will forgive you the first time, and the second time I may turn you over my lap and fan your, well where you set down. And the third time I will and all the times after that I may let Jesus punish you for all the mistakes do you understand."

And he let her go.

"Yes brother."

And with a big hug she turned to see and help repair his bed. Monday night they went to pick out the furniture that Alice would need for her new office. She got things that would make things flow better. Tuesday night they all went to pick out their bedroom furniture. Wednesday evening, they went and picked out the dining room furniture. Thursday night they went to the appliance store and got all the appliances they would need. The washer and dryer and refrigerator and microwave. Friday, they went to pick out new dishes and pots and pans silverware with all the towels and other rugs that they would need for the bathrooms. One thing they did not have to do is paint the house was all new paint and it was agreeable with them to leave it for the time being.

They all went to the house on Saturday afternoon and when they opened the door and Tom picked up Alice and carried her into the front entry. When Jody said, well what about me.

"Bill picked her up and carried her into the house and there was such a mess that they were in shock. The note on the door told them that it was all theirs and could move in anytime. As they were checking out the house. Tom put Alice down and gave her a kiss and Jody said.

"You can put me down but no kiss and welcome to this mess. "Why did they not clean up their mess I cannot believe this?"

Said Alice. As she walked through the lower rooms. The doorbell rang and Tom went to see who was calling so early. First nobody new they even bought this place yet.

"Hi, we are the cleaning people we are to give this place a good cleaning are you the new owners?"

"Yes, we are Tom and Alice Bay with Bill and Jody are children. We are just looking around, and we will stay out of your way."

"We understand that the refrigerator, washer and dryer are to be put into the garage. We will do that so we can clean behind them."

"Hey that is great when will you be done with your cleaning."

"We should be done by Monday after noon if everything goes well."

"We need to move my wife's office into the middle room upstairs can that be cleaned first so yet this afternoon we can have them deliver the office furniture."

"No problem it will be done first thing today do you want us to clean or do anything with the window curtains are you going to replace them. The only ones we want to keep are the ones in the living room and the downstairs bed room. The rest you can put in boxes and put them in the garage for now. Are you doing this for a living?"

"Yes, we are why?"

"Well, we have Alice's house that is sold and needs to be cleaned before next Saturday can you do that for us?"

"Yes, we can just tell us where it is and give us a key and leave a note hanging in the kitchen what you want us to do."

"Thank you and later we will have my house that we think we are going to have it for rental purpose, and it will also need a good cleaning as soon as we get it emptied and get rid of all the stuff."

"Just let us know and we will be right on it."

They left and stopped to see if Alice's furniture was ready to be delivered for her office on Monday after noon. The other places were told to deliver on Tuesday and Wednesday. By Friday they should have a livable home. Then they stopped for a rental moving truck.

"Bill, you can drive this can't you. We are going to load our garage and put it all in the pole barn and then when we have it all here, we will have an auction and get rid of all of it."

"You mean we are going to work on Sunday?" asked Jody.

"Yes, we are but we are still going to church and Sunday school, and with what we have been through the last few weeks I don't believe God will disown us for doing this on Sunday. I know our prayers have been answered this is okay with God. Bill take this truck to your house we will start loading that stuff first. We will go home and change into some old clothes and bring you some to change into also."

They were off and they had a very big job ahead of them. It was ten o-clock when they got home all dirty and tired and ready for some rest. Next morning Bill and Tom were loading the truck from the garage when Alice called.

"Guys it is time to get ready for church."

"We have to plan for Monday afternoon to move mom's office and get it reset up."

Tom, I forgot I need a special line for my computer setup."

"I will see in the morning when they install it we will have to use our cell phones and use the house line until they get to it probably."

"Do you think they can make it a special line?"

"I will ask now let's get to church."

They cleaned out the garage and most of the house things and it was late.

"Dad, Bill and I were thinking we could take off from school tomorrow to help finish up, and move mom's stuff what do you think?"

"How about in the afternoon we cannot do anything until afternoon and then when the furniture is placed, we can move all of mom's things for her office at once and restart the process so as she will not miss too much on line time. We must wait until she changes all the phone numbers and that we will know in the morning. So, I believe we can get her new office and her, placed by time to close her day."

"Great we can be here by twelve fifteen or do we go to the office first?"

"No Bill we will have to come here to change our clothes first and get something to eat."

"Oh, so that is what sisters are for."

"Well, that is what God gave us women to get men to help you make your decisions that is why he said we become one."

"Yea that is good for mom and dad, but we are not married so we are not one. I can think what I don't without asking you if it is okay or not."

"Now! Now! Children lets be nice and lovable remember our new way."

"Yea" said Jody as she gave Bill his big bear hug and a wet kiss on his cheek.

"Remember we are the weaker sex so be nice to your sister, and I can be silly, and I can always love you in a silly way."

"I think I have to go help dad I cannot win with the both of you."

By the end of the next week the two old homes were empty and cleaned they would work out if they still wanted to rent or sell Tom's house it was paid for and Tom thought they could do better renting it for more income and maybe it could be available for one of the kids if they decided to stay around here when and if they ever got married. Alice had her office all set up and running. The house was coming together and the date for the auction was in place for Saturday afternoon. Alice said as they were going to bed.

"Let's pray that all of our stuff God has someone who really needs it and it will all disappear Saturday."

"Dear heavenly father as we are now one and in a different place. Let us always remember that it was you who put his altogether. Let us always remember to thank you each day for the children and the difference in their lives. Thank you for the time we have together in this world we now live in. Help us to remember the bad times and not go back and reflect on them. We give them to you for the safe keeping that they need. To us they are just old baggage and is junk for someone else that thinks that they need it. Let this day of the sale be for us to remember of the good times we will have together out here in the country. Thank you for this new home you have so graciously given to us. Now as we sleep tonight, we ask for your safety for all of us and to be refreshed for the time tomorrow. In your precious name Jesus, we pray. A-men.

CHAPTER 20

Tom and Alice have been married for six months their home is the way they want it and school is to start in one month. They had decided to rent Tom's old house and they had a real nice couple with a small girl renting from them. Alice has picked up one more hospital so that kept her and Jody very busy with Bill helping when he was not helping with the outdoors work which he liked a lot more than the book work. Tom's job was going well, and he had been promoted so he had more pressure but less physical work. They had been addressing Bill and Jody about what they were going to do after this year of school and if college was in their future. Bill was going for sports to the small school if they wanted him but was not sure. Jody wanted to but she may just stay and help her mom in doing her work and swing if they could get more work from other resources.

"Jody, I think you should go to college and get a degree you may need it down the road."

Her dad was persistent in his request.

"I don't want to spend a lot of money and not know if it will help me do what I want to do."

"What do you want to do with your life?"

"I want to be the best mother and wife that God has ever put here on this earth. I want my kids to love me not resent me for the way they were treated."

"What about your husband will he be that way also."

"He will or I will not marry him."

"But daughter you must pick him before you get married and have children. So how will you know what or how he will act later when the children arrive?"

"Dad I will know God is going to answer my prayers I have asked him for years and I know he will not let me down, and I know he already has him picked out for me. I know that he will put us together in a certain place and then we will both know."

"Well, it seems you have your mind made up, and your heart and soul set on this idea."

"For now, yes, I have to start basketball warm ups as soon as school starts and I want to do my best this year. Maybe I will be asked to cheer lead again. Do you realize that in thirty days we will be back into the thick schedule again? Are you and mom ready for that to happen?"

"Yes, and now I can have time to be alone no work no kids just the two of us."

"Dad, are you kidding what about Bill and I don't you want to see us play?"

"We will see how it works out we still have some time to decide."

"Mom did you hear dad he wants to be with you instead of watching our games this year. Are you going to let him do that?"

"I think he is ribbing you just a little he would not miss your games for anything and that includes being home with me. Just don't pay any attention to that I have ways to get him there."

"Mom, do you see any change in my dad since you first knew him, and now that you have been married this long?"

"Yes, I see a very loving man who was hiding behind a very dark shadow that has now uncovered his light for others to see. I see him as a loving parent who has always put his child above all else and has a caring towards my son in the same way. I see a man who is dedicated to see that his children go forth and strive to be what God has planned for them since God who created them, and has given him the ability, and gave them to him and how to apply them to each child. I see a husband who cares for the woman God gave him including your mom, and I see that he expects to follow up to be the best husband that his wife will let him be. I see a man who puts God first in his life and then he himself second, and by that he upholds his responsibility to his wife and family. I see him make good decisions, but always ask for God's input before he goes forward. I see a man who loves his savior and father in heaven through the Holy Spirit, which is his interpreter of his soul. I am so glad that I found or he found me, and really thank God who brought us together through the two loveliest children we know. We owe it all to him that he used someone else like children to put us where we are today."

"Wow I never seen my dad as that, but I believe and know now that you have brought it out and showed me what a true lovely saintly woman you are and I am proud to call you my mom."

Summer went by too fast for Tom and Bill they spent a lot of time at the gulf and their pond fishing and had their freezer half full. They had stocked their pond so in two years they would have a lot of fish meaning very good times together. Jody and Alice worked hard to simplify the process of all the paperwork with the extra load, so Alice could half way keep up. This job became a family thing. Just before school started Alice told Tom he might have to help some during the weekends to help keep up. Tom called a meeting of the mines one evening.

"Well, I have one thing to say about the work load that my lovely wife has put us under and I have a saying I have not used it for some time. It goes like this does work enjoy what you do for it, or do you enjoy the work you do. Now before we go future into his discussion I need some input from you three people I love the most."

"I wonder if we need all that extra money?"

Said Bill.

"I don't know but I like the money I get from it, it makes me less dependent on my dad for money he has to pay for this new home."

Jody stated.

"I want to do my share in the providing for this family, and I may now be a little too happy because I have always had to do it all and still have some savings. It was hard for Bill and me when we started out all them years ago with someone else providing for us. Then little by little my work started to pay the bills except we never had anything to fall back on in an emergency. Maybe that makes me a little bit greedy to have a small nest egg put back so we cannot worry about the future."

"Them are all great responses. Now let me try to answer some of them to let us make a good rational decision. Bill wants to know if we need all the extra money. My answer is not that much. Jody likes the money, so she does not have to ask for any from us. My answer is if you are in school it is your parent's responsibility to support all your needs. Wrong way to look at it. Mom has struggled for a long time on what we say paycheck to paycheck and not knowing what she would do if she and Bill ever had an emergency, and she now wants a nest egg for that purpose. Good idea but I have been figuring out our finances after selling and buying and I am at a point that I can say what we now have. I know that God can take anyone of us at any given moment and we should leave our family in. Let's say this we are not on top of the world, but we are not at the bottom of the ocean either. The Bible says that we should save some for the future instead of spending all we get, as soon as we get it. Now this I can say for sure this home we now live in is all paid for. We need to make enough money to pay the taxes and insurance and whatever it takes to for upkeep it may need. I make more money now than when we were married. We have a rental house that is paid for and is bring in a monthly income. From the sale of your old home and with the combined moneys is what paid for this place? Now I have answered all your questions except one our nest egg. I have money placed in four o one K's at work and I have the company retirement plan of which I am one hundred percent invested. We now have about fifteen thousand dollars in the bank. We have two children who in one year will be starting college and with some grants and scholarships that would help, but if not then we will deal with it when the time comes. That should answer all your questions except what I want or need for the three people who I am responsible for I don't want my wife and kids to be working all night when I would rather be at a ball game watching them precipitate in what they enjoy doing. Since I am the head of this house, I hope that I will have a heavy say as to what we do. So, I am asking my wife my daughter and my son to make the decision as to how much she or he wants to give up for this one year of your workload. That will be my wife's decision and Jody's so they can do the work in a regular, period and not take away from anything the family would like to do. Keep in mind the four hundred dollars from the rental house is going into the savings. My salary pays the bills the money Alice and Jody makes is for her nest egg and for Jody to be happy. Bill, you get what we have left over at the end of the week and for the help that you give to your mom and Jody. Just make sure you choose wisely the accounts you can do the easiest and still make good hourly wages while doing them. So, it is up to Alice and Jody to make the last decision I and Bill will not get involved unless you need some help while making up your minds on what to give up. Does anybody have any questions, or have I covered all the thoughts towards which way we are going?"

"Thank you, my wise husband. Jody and I can make that happen in two weeks' l hope we should give them at least two weeks' notice if we are not going to work for them."

"Yes dad, but what if I don't go to college next year?"

"Right now, we think you should, and we have a whole year for you to convince us or give us good reasons why you do not need to go."

"It sounds good to me I have a sister I don't really know and all we do is watch each other at work we never have any time to have fun together so I am going with dad's ideas and if I can get some grants or scholarships, it will be from my good grades or playing of sports this last year of high school. I can't study and work every night with sports my grades will start falling off and that will just put more burden on the family budget."

"Okay girls the rest is up to you, and Jody keep yours to about ten hours a week if you can please."

CHAPTER 21

Bill is having his best year in football as quarterback for the team he has more confidence, and now there are college personal coming to watch him play. Jody is cheer leading and very proud of her brother for his efforts and loves him with all her heart. Yet Bill does not see how she feels and Jody cannot tell him her true feelings. Jody now only works two hours on wed evening and about six hours on Saturday afternoons. Tom is enjoying his time with his wife at the ball games he cannot talk enough about his son and his pride for what he is accomplishing. Sometimes Jody feels a little left out when Bill 's playing is all that they talk about. One Friday evening after the game they were having family time and it was Bill this and Bill that until Jody went to her bedroom and got her coat and came back saying.

"Guess I will go home see you tomorrow for work."

She went out the door and sit on the porch swing. After a while her dad came out to see what the problem was and where she was going so late.

"I was just put out I used to be part of this family and for the last few weeks all I hear is Bill this and Bill that and I figured if that was all it was about then I would find me a new home so maybe I would be noticed for what I do. Of course, all I do is cheer lead and run around in them skimpy clothes freezing my legs and arms off trying to get them guys to play harder to win. That's not very much and probably no one even notices so maybe it is time I gave it up, and please don't tell me you are sorry I don't like that word I have heard it enough times from you. I could finally understand if someone would just tell me. You have your son and wife so who needs me anymore I am just the little girl around here."

"Jody, I had no idea it was hurting you like this way I believe that the way you have been so excited about our family that you were happy you have never said anything."

"I am happy I would just like to be noticed by someone I have instead of by all the kids I don't really care about, they only like me because they get to see all legs clear up to my butt."

"Sweetheart come back inside and let's talk about this."

"No I don't want to talk to them about it I don't want to hurt their feelings and get this family all out of joint."

"What do you want me to do about it. Alice and I talk about how much better you are then most of the girls on your squad."

"How come you never let me know. Don't you think I need your approval?"

Then Jody starts crying. Tom sets down beside her and puts his arm around her.

"Jody, I feel like a big heal and a fool that my daughter sets here thinking that I don't care about her. That you think I have forgotten about your feeling unless you are playing ball. The rest and I are wrong and I am sure they will feel bad if they knew. I will try to remember to bring you into our talk time. Is that okay and is that all that is bothering you."

Tom pulled his daughter close to his chest and told her he still loved her and that he would do different.

"Dad I like the way this feels it has been a long time since you held me this way."

"Yes, I have forgotten."

"Dad can I trust you with something?"

"You mean can I keep a secret to myself?"

"Yes, I have a bigger problem and I don't know what to do about it. I am in love with my brother and I can't tell him and I don't want you to say anything to him or mom."

"Oh me! I see and I don't or can't tell you what to do about that. How long have you felt this way?"

"A long time I just kept telling myself he was just my friend, and now I don't know what to think."

"This will be our secret, and I will pray about it so maybe God will feed you the right answers just do not let it eat you up. Bill is not looking at anybody else is he that you know of?"

"No but all the girls are talking because he is the big football star and he will be the home coming king and some girl will be out there hanging on him as the queen what am I going to do I don't know."

"Is your name on the list for queen?"

"The list goes up Tuesday next week."

"Well how can we get your name on that list?"

"We can't I am his sister and that is against the rules."

"Here wipe those eyes and let's go in it is getting late. Bill has already gone to bed and Alice will be waiting for me."

"Please do not say anything okay dad. I feel better and I know you will not forget and I believe you will bring up my name some too. It is alright to do what you do for Bill he needs your input he really likes you, and I don't want to break up anything that is between you two. You go on in I will be in, in a minute good night dad I truly love you and I am glad you are my dad."

"Thanks, I love you also."

Jody set looking at the stars wondering how her life got so serious with Bill what had she been thinking falling in love with her brother what would people think. Bowing her head, she talks to her Heavenly Father for comforting times ahead.

"Dear Lord God, in heaven what have I done why am doing this to myself and even could ruin my dad and mom and my brother. Please show me a way out of this. Help me to change my mind. Have something come between us. If this is not your will for me. Lord I love you and need your power in my life to overcome. Turn Bill loose from my mind to do his will for you and let me not hold him back. Keep my thoughts away from him so I can go on with my life, as you want it. Help me to understand and forget how I feel about the way he looks and acts around me, and others that I have no control over. Lord he is not mine so I have no control over his actions and or what he believes he is to do. He is yours and I now turn lose all thoughts about who he is and that I want him for myself. I will wait for the one you have for me to be a part of or you say leave my mother and father and be joined as one with my husband. If Bill is not your choice for me then take him from my mind and leave him only as my brother and nothing else. Please show me a way to do this Lord. I love you so and I want your will for me only. I ask this in your precious name A-men."

Jody gets up and goes to bed to wake in the morning for work she is very quiet for a long time only saying good morning to her dad and mom not saying anything to Bill. At lunch, she did not stop working. She didn't even answer when they called to ask if she was hungry. When Alice came back from eating she asked.

"Jody, you seem to be somewhere, a long way from us. Is there anything I can help you with?"

Her answer was.

"No! I am just thinking."

"Well when you want to talk I will listen. I have not seen you like this since I have known you. Even your dad seems worried about how you are."

"There is nothing wrong with me I said I am thinking and working."

"Okay then I will not bother you."

Alice left the office and went outside to enjoy the warmth of the sun on the porch. She didn't know if she had done something to Jody or said something wrong, and she had to know but she didn't want to tread where she didn't belong.

"Lord Jesus help me to understand what my daughter is going through."

CHAPTER 22

The school year ended with Jody and Bill graduating and Bill had top honors for the boys with his grades and sports letters and records. Jody had her sports records and letters and a four-point 0 grade with only five others with that high of grades. She was not honored like Bill was in front of the school and their community. She had made up her mind that it did not make her a better person or a worst person, and she did not have to return to the school or even the community. She was through with school, and it would be a long summer until Bill left for the college, he was to play ball for. Jody had pulled back just to work she always had some excused as to not go on family outings she had talked Alice into getting more work for her after school. That would keep her very busy and out of their lives they could up and do as they please and so could Bill. There was a very dark shadow that hung over the family and Jody was the cause of it, but no one wanted to ask her because she had turned the temper up to hot when confronted about what she was doing.

"Jody, this is your dad do you remember him?"

"Why do you ask?"

"Because Alice thinks she must walk on eggshells just to be around you. I want you to tell her what is wrong to ease the tension in that office you know it is her doing that makes it possible for you to work. So, I am asking you nicely to break the cage and come on out and be the person you used to be. If not, then pick a school that you want to go to. You cannot make her life miserable because you can't face life like you want it."

"Are you telling me to shape up or get out?"

"No, I am asking you to be the polite person that I know you can be. I am asking you to quit upsetting this family we have put up with it for far too long. If I still know your problem, I think it is time you face up to it. Do not ruin your family because of what you think is love for you and you can't reach it. It's maybe that because of your attitude it is running away. It is like I hear some of your friends and school kids. Get a life and quit messing up ours. If you have and old sore then let it heal. If you can't do it then we can get you some counseling. I just want you to know everyone in this family loves you, but you seem to be trying to drive us all away. I feel sometimes I should do what I never had to do all your life."

"And what is that."

"Turn you across my knees, and tan your, rear-end to get your brain chemicals back in adjustment."

"You wouldn't dare, would you?"

"I said I didn't want to, but something is going to give and it is you that is the something. I think that you owe everyone an apologize and start with a different focus starting now. Your brother is leaving in three days for school he will be gone nine months before he returns, we will be going to see his home games. You can come along if you get it right if not we will go without you. You are beginning to act just like your mother, and I am asking you to change course before you are just like her, all alone in life. Do you understand, I know you do and I have tried to help I kept your secret and I will not tell it even now. I am asking you to face your life that only you can make it seem that you have sidestepped Jesus and are on the wrong path going against the grain. Now give me a hug and go cry your pain away I will see you at dinner."

"Tom, do you know where Jody is she doesn't seem to be here?"

"I had a heart-to-heart talk with her and she is probably somewhere crying about it."

"You weren't mean about it, were you?"

"No, I just told her she needed to change and quit trying to keep the family stirred up."

"Maybe I need to go talk with her we used to be friends, but I know she has pulled away from me. After I eat I will go talk to her."

"Bill maybe you can help her with her problem. I will try mom is that okay with you dad if I try?"

"No, you go ahead but keep your good side out."

Bill eats and excuses himself and starts walking. He does not call her name he is just looking. After checking the pole barn and around the house decides to go to the pond. After getting close he sees her lying in the sand they had hauled in to make a small beach area. As he approaches her, she turns her head to see whom, and then asks.

"And what do you want if I am in your place then I will move away?"

"Jody, I came to see if you were hungry dinner has been waiting for you."

"I don't want anything."

Then she sets up and turned her back to him.

"Jody, I do not know what I did, but we used to be friends and now I don't even know you or why you have turned away from me and the dad and mom who loves you."

"Don't tell me about love and friends."

I didn't come here to upset you I am leaving in two days and I wanted us to part still friends, but you have told me you don't need me so I will just leave."

"You do that run away you don't know anything about true friendship or love or anything all you care about is that my dad took you in and you took him away."

"Jody that is not true."

"Just go I do not like you and do not want you to talk to me so just leave."

Bill is stumped at the way Jody is trashing him. He started to say something, but just turned and walked back to the house. Jody came in and went straight to her room. When it got dark. The next morning, she went only to the office. She was afraid to come to breakfast, but did not move, she talked to Alice about work but that was all. She stayed involved in her work all day. In the evening, Alice told her she was fixing a special dinner for Bill as a going away home meal because he would not be getting meals like it for a long time.

"Mom I won't be eating I have got to finish this work I don't know why I am so far behind, but it has to be done today, or I will lose that company's work."

Jody was absent from the meal Bill said nothing and Tom just eat in a quite space only talking when he was asked something. Jody worked late and went to the kitchen after all was in bed to get something to eat then went to her room. The next morning Bill is talking at the table saying,

"I am going away, and I have lost my best friend I thought I had, and I don't know what I did to make her not like me. She jumped all over me last night down by the pond. She told me I didn't have a clue about friendship or family love, and she didn't want to ever see me again and to just leave. She told me I got what I wanted by taking her place with her dad and I should be happy about it. I guess I don't understand, but dad I did not take her place with you, did I?"

"No, you have done nothing wrong that I know of it is something she is struggling with and even I cannot help her least now."

"Well guys we have to leave to be at the bus station in one half hour so go get your things in the car Bill while I clean up the table."

"And I will go and talk with Jody."

Tom knocked on Jody's door to get no answer he tried the door and called her name, but still no answer. He stepped into the room to find Jody looking out the window in her robe.

"Jody, may I come in?"

She turned and looked at her dad.

"I guess you can what do you want I am not hungry, and I need to get dressed and go to work."

"You get dressed and come downstairs we are going to take your brother to the bus station as a whole family do you get what I just said there is nothing else going on you have thirty minutes to show up."

With that Tom backs out of the room. Jody mumbles to herself (I will go but you can't make me like it). She arrives as they are leaving for the car to join them. She rides to the bus station saying not one word. When they arrive, Bill takes his bag to the bus, and they are all standing talking except Jody is hanging back about three feet. They announce the bus is leaving in ten minutes and everyone is to be boarding. Bill goes to his mom and while hugging her he says.

"Mom thanks for this part of my life I will miss you and I love you and will pray for Jody every night."

Then he goes to Tom and puts his arms around him telling him.

"Thanks for believing in me and I hope you and mom can get Jody to snap back from wherever she is I will miss our time together, and I love you, you are the only dad I will ever know or have."

He turns to Jody and walks up to her to give her a goodbye hug, but she would not look at him.

"Jody, I am unhappy for you, and I feel it is my fault that you do not like me anymore, but you are my sister and will always be my sister and through thick and thin I will never forget the times we have had together. In my mind, you are still my friend that I cannot forget what we had and someday I may find why it all ended. I can tell you with a sad heart I will miss you and I do love you."

With that he turned and entered the bus with a backwards wave goodbye. Jody turns with tears in her eyes and ran back to the car. Tom and Alice waited until they could not see the bus any longer than they returned to the car, after one week there was a letter come from Bill it was addressed to Jody. She left it lay on the entry way table until Tom took it to her desk. She put it beside her computer and never opened it. This would be one of many.

CHAPTER 23

Jody got a letter from Bill at the first of every month and they got stuck besides her computer, and never opened. After Christmas Alice asked why she did not return Bill's letters. Her dad told her to grow up and at least read them and it won't hurt to write him. One evening at the dinner table Alice said she got a letter from Bill and he was not coming home for the summer he got a job at the college and he could keep in shape at the gym, and he would try to come home before school classes started in the fall. He says he has found a good friend and she has helped him through some tuff tests. Jody slammed her fork down and asked to be excused and went to her room. Tom and Alice just watched her walk away then Alice said.

"WHAT WAS THAT ALL ABOUT?"

"Hon, it is time we had a talk I promised I would keep this secret, but all it is doing is separating us as a family."

"What secret and why is it kept from me?"

"Our daughter has been in love with her brother for over two years and she cannot tell him she does not know how to handle it and is afraid people will talk if she lets it out. She does not want to hurt Bill but is being eaten up inside because of it."

"Oh, my word this has been her problem all this time?"

"I am afraid so, I have talked to her several times and prayed about it for her, but nothing has changed."

"That is why she does not read his letters, and is upset every time we talk about how he is doing, and why she would not go to any of his games. Oh, Tom what can we do to help her get through she will self-destruct if she does not get help."

"No I believe she is stronger than that it just has to come to a head someday."

"Do you care if I confront her about Bill?"

"No as long as you keep the secret a secret unless she decides to bring it up."

Next day Alice and Jody were working and Alice asked her.

"Jody how do you feel is something we can talk about like we used to not so long ago?"

"I am fine I have been under so much pressure for the last year that I thought I was going crazy for a while but I am coming out of it."

"Was there something I did or said last night that upset you."

Jody did not answer but turned her head so mom could not see the tears that were starting to come into her eyes.

"If there was I now wish I had not said it, but I would like to know so I won't upset you again."

"Mom it is not anything you or dad does it is just that for so long all I hear is Bill this and Bill that until I think I am just a worker here."

Alice turn to be quite for a while.

"Is that what is upsetting you all the time, and if it is so we cannot talk about Bill when you are around I thought that we were a family and I thought family share all our concerns so we could pray and talk about them instead of holding them in then feel bad about it. I think that it is something deeper when we are talking about Bill. The reason is why you have ten letters from Bill right there and you have not read one of them or written him back. I thought you two were friends that is not the way you treat your friends. So now would you like for me to guess things or do you want to open up your heart and share what is wrong between you two."

"It is not what you think mom so just leave it be."

"I got a letter about three months ago from Bill and he told me what you said down at the pond before he left. Do you remember that and what makes you think that he took your dad away from you? Even I have not done that he thinks more of you then any one of us. I see you give him looks and snap at him asking enough that I have wanted to scold you for it, but I have stayed out of it. I know a young girl just like you and she was really upset most of her time in high school. Her problem was she was very much in love with a certain boy and he would not give her the time of day. Her mom found out about it and went to the boy to see if he had any other girl or if he had any feeling towards her daughter. He had liked her a lot but he could not stay that way because of the way she acted so he had almost forgotten about how she used to be and that is when he really like her. That girl acted just like you. We are humans and we have a canny act of hurting the ones we love the most. Do you want me to keep guessing or shut up?"

"Mom did my dad talk to you?"

"We talk to each other a lot what, was he supposed to talk to me about."

"I told him a secret and I wondered if he told you about what it was about."

"I don't think so, but if you want me to know then you will have to tell me."

"Mom I am such a fool I don't want to hurt you or dad and I sure don't want to hurt Bill. I guess I act pretty bad and I use Bill and you guys to keep me mad or not showing how I feel."

"And, tell me Jody don't you think we can help or do you not want our help at all."

Jody broke down and the tears flooded her eyes and big sobs came from her throat."

Jody dear this breaks my heart and I cannot help you unless you tell me what has been haunting you for so long."

"I want to but I can't it will put us in a problem that will affect my life and I can't tell you yet some day maybe I will be able to do it."

"Jody, I will pray that Jesus can save you from the hurt that you carry, but I have to ask you don't hurt Bill and I anymore for this. It will someday hurt your father and my relationship and I know you don't want that to happen, do you?"

"I will figure it out soon I don't want to lose you or my dad. You two are meant to be together God choose you to be one and I cannot stay around if I am causing you both trouble if so then I would have to leave."

"Do you think that with you leaving it would solve this problem and not affect your dad and my relationship. Jody, you are nineteen years old you have to try being a grown up by now, don't you think I am right?"

"I am grown up I just don't like what I have grown up into."

"I have to go fix dinner your dad will be home soon, and there is another letter down stairs for you. Yes, it is from Bill."

"I will get it at dinner time do you want me to help you?"

"You could set the table if you would like too."

"I will be down in a minute to do that."

As she was setting the table the phone rang.

"Hello yes I will get her. Mom you are wanted on the phone."

"Hi mom was that Jody?"

"Yes, and how are you, about four thirty great. I have to finish dinner see you then."

As she hangs up the phone she shouts a "Thank you Lord Jesus."

CHAPTER 24

"Tom, I got a phone call from an old friend he is coming here Friday evening we need to pick him up at four thirty can you do it for me."

As she winked at him

"I don't think I can get away that early and you have a conference call at that time."

"Yes, so Jody can I ask you to do that for me it sure would make my day."

"Yes, I can do that how will I know him he will know you from the family picture, and now I can relax thank you Jody I appreciate this very much you can take my van when you go."

Jody never thought any more about it until Friday her mom said Jody it is four o-clock you had better go or you will be late to the bus station."

"Oh, mom I forgot all about going I will be off.

As she rushed out the door forgetting the van keys and having to return for them.

"What's wrong?"

"I forgot the keys."

"Okay drive carefully."

"I will."

Jody arrives at the station and get out of the van and goes inside to see if the bus has arrived as it pulled into the driveway. She decided she would wait inside to stay out of the traffic of people. When she looked up again, there Bill was coming through the door. He turned and saw her with a hand up he says.

"Hello sis how are you did you come alone."

"Just get in the van and don't speak."

"Hey what is wrong with you never mind give me the keys."

"I drove here and I drive home now get in."

"You see that cop I am going to call him over here and tell him you stole my mom's van."

"I did not steal anything and if you want a ride then you had better get in."

"Hey officer."

"You idiot what is your problem, give me the keys and get in the other side."

"Okay"

As she threw the keys at him and climbed in the back of the van. When they arrived home, Jody jumped out of the van and went straight to her room without saying anything to Alice.

"Mom what is wrong with that stupid sister I have, someone should let me in on this bashing I have been taking from her before I slap her silly. Never mind just keep her away from me. I come home for two days just to see you and dad. I must leave Sunday afternoon. Is dad home yet?"

"No but he will be here by the time you take your case up to your old room."

"Is that hell cat up there I don't want to be around her she has lost her mind or something."

"Be nice Bill even if she isn't."

"Okay mom just for you I love you."

Bill goes to his old room and drops his bag noticing Jody in the office with the door partially open as he walks by he grabs the knob and slams the door, and goes back down stairs.

"Hi dad good to see you how have you been I had two days it has been tuff with the work and my workouts for football. I wanted to come and bring you the game schedule and your honorary tickets for home games. I got a good price on them. All upper-class men get them I only got two since Jody doesn't like to watch me anymore."

"Well that is great can I pay you for them. No, you pay a low fee at the gate with these tickets. I think it is five dollars apiece."

"Great hon. we have the cheap seat tickets."

As he patted Bill on the back.

"Come in it is time to eat it has been a long time since you have had a good old home cooked meal."

"You can say that all I get is hospital food at school. It tastes bad but it works gives me the stamina to keep me going."

"Tom go get Jody time to eat."

"Jody, it is time to eat are you ready."

"I will be down in about ten minutes I have a program that is just about finished then I have to sign off. Go ahead and start without me."

By the time, Jody gets to the table everyone else is through so she fills her plate and goes into the kitchen so Alice can clear the table. She asked Jody in the kitchen.

"Are you okay?"

"No why did you not tell me that I was picking up Bill."

"I wanted to see just how much you hated him, and I knew if I told you he would have to set in the bus station for about one hour to be picked up by your dad or me when I got through with my phone call."

"Okay you are forgiven, but next time I will leave him there and come back home."

"Jody, just never mind it is your problem and I don't want to help you get through it I give up you just keep on hurting, but you will be nice to him and your dad and me while you are in this house. Do I make myself clear? It is okay for you and your dad to keep secrets but not me. I am upset and I don't care who knows it."

As she left Jody setting at the bar with her mouth open. Bill brings a hand full of dishes to the kitchen and leaves without looking at Jody he did not want to get chewed on again. Jody stayed in her room and worked without speaking to anyone the whole weekend when Tom and Alice took Bill to the bus station he did not even tell her goodbye. After the bus left Tom was told what happened between Alice and Jody and what Jody had told Bill in the car in the way from the bus station. Tom was at a loss he had to stop this at whatever cost it would take. When they arrived home, Tom told Alice

"I am going up to talk to Jody and give her one last chance to go straight or to get out and make her own way I have had enough of this it is coming between us and that is not going to happen."

"Tom be careful with what you say."

When he knocked on her door she asked.

"What do you need?"

"I need to talk to you now."

"I am not dressed."

"You got two minutes then I am coming in."

"Okay dad I am ready."

"Set down and listen to me I am going to tell you this one time and then you will have a choice. I have never been so upset with anyone in my life as I am with you and your behavior and I am not going to put up with it any longer it is time you get started acting you real age. You have upset this whole family that I wanted to be happy, but because of your stupidity things has gotten out of control. We have put up with it for over a year and you don't want to know what I really want now, but you are still my only daughter and you bring back all the memories that I had forgotten about with your mother and if you must be this way then you will be just like her maybe she would take you in if you can find her. In three weeks, we are going to Bill's first football game and you are going with us and you only have two choices you go with us or you go on your own. I am the head of this family and you are going to follow the rules or you can head, your own home and do as you see fit. If you think I am being harsh then so be it. Do you understand what I have just told you? Never mind I don't want you to lie to me by saying yes and then going on the same way."

Tom got up and left the room without another word. Jody set there and then lay down and cried herself to sleep. The next three weeks they moved around and spoke only when needed. On Friday evening at dinner Tom said.

"We are leaving at eight o-clock in the morning to go watch Bill's game."

He said no more. Alice and Jody cleared the table and washed their dishes and Tom went to his study. Before Jody went upstairs she went to the study to talk to her dad.

"May I see you for a little while dad?"

"What do you want from me?"

"Nothing but to hear me out I have thought since the last time you talked to me that I would leave and get me a job and place to live. Except that would only hurt you and make me the person I knew. I know you don't like the word sorry, but I am and I will be ready to go with you in the morning. I will respect you and mom and Bill I will keep my thoughts to myself and someday maybe Bill will find his wife and then I will know I lost all my chances with him and it will be only my fault and I will never bring you a grandchild. I am asking you to forgive me for all the trouble I caused you and mom maybe someday I will ask Bill to do the same."

"Come here and they fell into each other's arms and he said.

"I accept and I am very sorry that I could not help you go through this, but I think you will be stronger for it."

"Hey, you two that is my place to be in your father's arms, but I can give a little for our daughter."

Jody went to Alice and gave her a hug also.

"I am sorry mom I will see you in the morning."

Eight o-clock they were on the road they would get to see Bill for about thirty minutes before he had to suit up for the game. When they arrived, they went to the study and literary where Bill was to be waiting. When he saw, them coming he ran to meet then with his friend.

"Hi mom and dad I want you to meet the second most, smartest girl I have ever known she is helping we with my studies and I owe her a lot for what she has done for me. This is Tonya and this is my sister Jody."

"Hi and I must say you have a very beautiful sister I would like to get to know her better, but I have to go help John with his next test glad to meet you."

"Don't pay much attention to Tonya she is what we call a lesbian she is after all the good-looking girls, but she is smart and I would be in trouble if she wasn't helping me."

Bill gives his mom a big hug and one for his dad.

"Bill be careful with Jody I know what her problem is and I and sworn to secrecy, but her problem is that and doesn't let on very much, but is very much in love with you and has been for as long as she has known you. Good to see you I sure miss them hugs."

Then he turns to Jody and said.

"Hi sis and Tonya is right I do have a very beautiful sister and I have missed her for a long time. May I have a hug from an old friend it would help me in my playing today."

Jody did let him hug her and she did partially put her arms loosely around him. As he backs up he said.

"Thanks, but we have to walk and talk I have ten minutes to get to the dressing room. Did you bring you cheap seat tickets, and here is a free one for my sister I am very glad you decided to come."

With that he left on the run so as not to be late.

"Well let's go get us a hotdog and soda and find our seats I want to see just where we will be setting."

They eat and found their seats, which was on the forty-yard line four rows up. "I like that boy of ours he has a good mind to get us seats this good."

The game started and Bill's team went down the field in four plays and scored it was a good game after that at half time the score was Bill's team up by fourteen points.

"Do you ladies need to go to the rest room or get something more to drink? We have about twenty minutes before play begins."

"They all jumped up and went Tom got the sodas and met them back at their seats. The players were coming back on the field and when the noise went down the announcer said. "

Everyone quite please I have a message for someone and this is very highly unusual I have never done this before. The message reads form the quarter back of our team. It says, (I love you Jody). I don't know about this Jody girl but she has to be pretty happy about now."

Jody looked at her mom and dad with as flushed face and tears in her eyes, but said nothing. Alice patted her on the shoulder and said.

"You know God he does some strange things, but he knows when to bring the best out in some one."

After the game and most all were gone this three of a family of four set basting in the wonderment of God's Grace. Jody said,

"Would you pray for me?"

"Our daughter we would be glad to pray for you.

"Dear Father in Heaven as we set here on this most wonderful day. We ask your love and blessings upon the children that you gave us let Jody feel your present's and let her have peace to come to her body and soul. Let love be for real and that it would be a glory unto your name. I her mother thanks you that truth has been awakened in all of us. May you protect her in the coming days? In your name, I pray. A-men"

"Thank you Lord for my daughter her special gift from you so many years ago. Thank you for my wife and the love she has for our daughter and for our son who has pulled himself up from such a place to stand tall among the men like here today. Thank you for this family and what we can do for you in the future. A-men."

"When we wait long enough my daughter isn't love grand and two day that dark shadow has been lifted from this family. We love you Jesus for believing in us. Let us do the same and believe in you, and the work set before us to do."

EPILOGUE

When this story started, it was a very happy beginning of what was to be a happy family. But as usual the people change as they go through life. Most of the time one is very hurt and sometimes more. It is hard to pull out of such deep depressing time for some and not for others. This family took a long time and for probably all the wrong reasons to start with, but in the process, they find peace and happiness. If you have never been a child who is torn with the grief of not having the love of one or, both parents that God gave you too. To not be able to understand why one is so good and the other so bad. A child who has given up hope, and only finds true love in one of their parents, and only bad from the other one. Can you imagine the pain of the heart to go through such a life? A child who must reach out to someone else to find the need that such child is missing. To find peace with another child of their same or the opposite sex. The course a child must follow to understand the hurt that lives within its own soul. To try to understand the purpose that God put them here for. The trouble trying to understand why to find that it is the parent's responsibility to give that child the help of understanding God's will in their life. To find out a lot of their problems through the life of a friend's parent or the new step parent that loves them and not knowing why such should happen to them. As this was written I tried to place myself in the heart of such a child. Not knowing the true feelings that I should have had, but foreseeing on the Bible and the truth that God has for us to live by. The girl Jody struggled with her real mother, but loved her father because that was where her true love came from. She was looking for someone who would be like her father and found a friend in Bill. His mother came to help her with emotions of what a woman should feel and how to handle those feelings. These four-people knowing God and believing in Jesus Christ became a real family. They had their ups and downs like all people when put into a certain room and knowing what to do still have thoughts that do not belong there. Their pasts have not jelled into the present yet, but are still the platform of their lives. They struggle and in the end when the head of the home stands up and acts as such the family forgets their own little problems and were united into a loving caring family. As you read this story I pray that you feel and hear Gods calling in your life to make it right with Jesus help and the commitment you have established in, and from the start.

THE END

BOOK REVIEW

Information for the writer to make changes or leave as is in his future books

Didyouenjoyreadingthisbook_____Why_____

Very much_____Moderately_____

What influenced your decision to purchase this book

Cover__Title__Price__Friends__Publicity__Back cover__By chance__Other__

Please check your age

Under 18__18-24__25-34__35-45__46-55__55 and over__

How many hours do you read per week_____

Name_____Occupation_____

Address_____City_____

State_____Zip_____

E-Mail_____

I will enjoy hearing from you.

Have you read other books from William Bradbury. Which ones and did you enjoy.

_____

E-Mail bradbury.william@yahoo.com.

Printed in the USA
CPSIA information can be obtained
at www.ICGtesting.com
CBHW051600041024
15321CB00062B/2859

9 781684 868841